Love is
a time of enchantment:
in it all days are fair and all fields
green. Youth is blest by it,
old age made benign: the eyes of love see
roses blooming in December,
and sunshine through rain. Verily
is the time of true-love
a time of enchantment—and
Oh! how eager is woman
to be bewitched!

DR. SHAW'S SECRETARY

Left in charge of her cousin's two young daughters while their parents are abroad, Clare Drury is relieved when her sister Alison, a children's nurse, arrives to help. As secretary to Dr. Raymond Shaw and novelist Ewan Burnett, Clare's time and emotions are divided. When one of the children falls ill Dr. Shaw visits regularly. And it is Alison who is thrown much in contact with the doctor . . .

KAY WINCHESTER

DR. SHAW'S SECRETARY

Complete and Unabridged

ULVERSCROFT
Leicester

First Large Print Edition
published December 1989

British Library CIP Data

Winchester, Kay, *1913–*
Dr. Shaw's secretary—Large print ed.—
Ulverscroft large print series: romance
I. Title
823′.914[F]

ISBN 0-7089-2114-0

Published by
F. A. Thorpe (Publishing) Ltd.
Anstey, Leicestershire
Set by Rowland Phototypesetting Ltd.
Bury St. Edmunds, Suffolk
Printed and bound in Great Britain by
T. J. Press (Padstow) Ltd., Padstow, Cornwall

1

RAYMOND SHAW pulled up in the lane above The Splash, and waited in the layby, while Clare Drury strode over the last few yards of the field path, climbed the stile and half slithered down the slope to the road.

All the fields one side of the road above Rexmundham were high, and those the other side lay low, swooping down to the woods and the river.

Up here the wind was fresh and keen, blowing away the early blossoms of thorn hedge and briar, scattering a pale pink carpet of wild cherry across the dusty surface, whipping colour into Clare Drury's normally pale cheeks and tearing back her immaculate black hair from the small ears until it was no more than a close cap hugging her head. Her brown eyes shone with the glow of health but her smile was purposely restrained because she dare not betray how glad she was to see him.

"I suppose," he remarked, leaning over and opening the door, "you'd rather finish your walk home being wind-blown, than accept a lift from me?"

Her face flushed with pleasure.

"Of course not, doctor! I'd love a lift," she said as she got in beside him. "Have you finished your rounds?"

"Have I what?" he repeated. "Of course not. I had four more calls after you went home today. I was going to look in on the Sims' child, anyway, but dear Miss Maggs is just fussing again, and old Tyler wants more pills."

"Can I drop them in for you to save you the visit?" she asked him quickly.

"No, it's all right. You get along home. Just come from Burnett's place, I suppose?"

She nodded. "You don't *mind*, do you? About me working for Mr. Burnett, I mean?"

"No. Why should I? What you do with your afternoons is your concern so long as you don't knock yourself up before surgery next morning," he was quick to say. Yet he sounded displeased. Ewan Burnett was not a patient of his. He was

2

a newcomer from London, author of five successful novels; a man who ignored the rest of the district until he needed a part-time typist.

"You know I meant it when I offered to come in and help with evening surgery," she reminded him.

"And I told you it wasn't necessary. Anyway, my father likes to take three of the evening surgeries, and you know he always prefers to work alone." He glanced at her as he straightened out after creeping round the rising bend at Farthingbridge Heights. "Is Burnett working you too hard? You're looking a bit peaky."

"No, of course not," she denied, perhaps a shade too quickly.

She liked the work in the big house on the hill and she had needed the extra money. She didn't want the doctor to think she was being worked too hard by someone else, but, at the same time, she was pleased that he noticed her. Usually she was no more to him than someone in a white coat who let in the morning patients and wrote up his card index and notes.

"Have you heard from your sister lately?

3

Not worried about her, are you?" Raymond Shaw asked, suddenly.

"I haven't heard lately," Clare confessed, "but I expect she's too busy to write. She's on the point of getting engaged, and there are exams and things. She's practically a qualified children's nurse now."

"And she's going to waste her training and get married!" he said, pointedly, as they swooped down into the outskirts of Rexmundham, past the old church with the round tower, and into the High Street.

"No, it won't be wasted. She hopes to go on working and, anyway, they won't be marrying for quite a while. Alison's Keith hasn't qualified yet and then there's his full year as a houseman before he sets up in practice somewhere." She smiled, her face lighting up as she talked of her sister. "You don't know Alison—she's too fond of children ever to waste that training."

"I may not have met the young lady but I feel I know her already, from the glowing descriptions you've given me of her," Raymond Shaw said, pulling up at the end of Clare's road. "Don't be late for surgery tomorrow—I suppose you've brought home loads of manuscripts to correct this evening?"

"Why?" she asked, quickly. "Did you want me to do something for you?"

"Yes—relax. Get a rest. Go out somewhere. Be young and care-free for once," he exploded. Then he looked bothered, as if he hadn't meant to say that. "Don't mind me—the parents of the Sims' child always get me rattled and I'm spoiling for another session. That poor brat doesn't stand a chance with a fussing mother like that. See you tomorrow, Clare," and he let in the clutch and roared away before she could answer.

Clare's married cousin, Susan, came to the door and opened it.

"Was that Dr. Shaw giving you a lift home?" she asked, smiling broadly.

"It was, but I almost wish I'd walked all the way," Clare said, grimly, following her cousin inside.

"In a mood, was he?" Susan asked, sympathetically. "Never mind. What that poor man has to put up with is no one's business. But isn't he good-looking? I didn't realise it until this afternoon. I had to call on him to see Mellie."

"Mellie! Why—what happened? He didn't mention it."

"Nothing serious—just a nasty grazed knee, but you know what she's like. She fell down on the concrete and got dirt in it. It needed cleaning up and she won't let me do anything like that. Still, Dr. Shaw managed all right. Had her eating out of his hand by the time he was finished. He's terribly good with children, isn't he?"

"I know," Clare agreed.

"Funny he never married. He's really quite young and attractive. I hadn't realised before. You know how one gets used to seeing a person around—he's just someone holding a little black bag and driving a two-toned car until you get a really close personal look at him and then he really is something!"

"He'd be flattered," Clare said, drily, turning away as she always did when Dr. Shaw was mentioned, so that no one should notice the way her cheeks burned and a glow came into her dark eyes. It wasn't right to get so worked up about someone you were employed by, she told herself angrily.

"You don't make the most of your

chances," Susan said, thoughtfully. "If I worked every morning with him as you do, I'd have had him dating me by now."

"Probably, but I'm not like you," Clare retorted. "Besides, I sometimes think one has less chance, working closely with a man—one becomes a part of the furniture and fittings. I'm sure he never really sees me. Where's Mellie now? Can I go and see her?"

"No, leave her alone, Clare. She's asleep—Jayne too," Susan said. "Besides, I wanted to talk to you about something else."

She sauntered over to the settee and perched on one arm; a rather plain but extremely well-groomed young woman who made up for lack of good looks by clever dress sense and more than her fair share of allure. No one looking at her would take her for the mother of two small children. Susan never allowed herself to be seen messy and untidy, no matter what the demands of the day had been.

"The most frustrating thing's happened. Tony rang up just after lunch. He's had the offer of a lifetime!" she said, torn between gloom and suppressed excitement. "His firm's giving him a job that will take him through France and Italy finishing up in North Africa."

"Sue, how marvellous!" Clare was genuinely thrilled for her cousin. "Big money in it?"

"Money? Yes, loads—but the utterly maddening part is, his boss says I can go too—in fact, he went so far as to say it might be better if Tony had his wife with him—entertaining and all that. Only how in the world can I?"

"But why not, Sue?"

"Think, Clare; what would I do about Jayne and Mellie?" She spread her hands in a dramatic gesture. "Tony is fed up about it, too! I've never made an issue of the children in their lives before, but they are definitely a stumbling block at this moment."

"Oh, Sue! But surely there's some arrangement you could make for Jayne and Mellie—someone who'd look after them? What about Mrs. Newsome next door?"

"No, I thought of that at once but I forgot one small thing—her three have measles!"

"Oh, that settles that. Well, what about Mrs. Brown next door the other way?"

"They wouldn't want to stay with her. You know what she's like—don't do this, don't touch that! I had tears from them at the very thought of it."

"Oh, what a shame," Clare said, worriedly, "I was thinking that if someone could look after them in the daytime, I'd be here at night."

Susan stared at Clare. "Would you? Would you mind taking them on, honey? It'd be rather a drag, seeing to their clothes and baths and everything—"

Clare grinned happily. "Oh, come now, I know they play me up sometimes, but I'd manage somehow. How long would you expect to be away?"

"A month at least," Susan said.

"Oh!" Clare murmured. "That's different, isn't it? I mean *I* don't mind the evenings and nights, but who would we get for the daytime? A day nursery's no good because of week-ends and the surgery."

"It's no good, I just can't go!" Susan said, her tones flattened with such deep disappointment that Clare looked sharply at her. Before she could suggest anything else, however, someone opened the front gate and came up the path.

"It's someone from the end house—the new people," Clare said. "I'll go, shall I?"

She came back almost at once, carrying a letter.

"It's for me from Alison. I wondered why she hadn't written. It's been lying under their hallstand for a week—they've only just got round to clearing up and putting a basket for mail on their door. How is it possible that it's always the letters one is waiting for that get wrongly delivered?" she muttered wrathfully, curling up in the armchair and preparing to read it.

Susan said, "I'll make some tea. I could do with a cup," and she trailed out to the kitchen. She didn't know what she had hoped that Clare could suggest, by way of answer to her problem, but Clare was so resourceful that you never knew what ideas she could produce at a moment's notice.

When she went in with the tray Clare was sitting reading the letter through again.

10

"Poor Alison, what am I going to do for her?" Clare said, putting the letter down. "You know that nice Keith Everton that she was going to be engaged to? Well, they've broken it off," she said, referring to the letter again. "Alison's making light of it and saying that she doesn't think he was right for her and all that. But I think she's covering up. It must have been a pretty big row. She seems awfully upset underneath, in spite of her babbling on about getting through her exams all right, and being qualified at last."

"Oh, help," Susan exclaimed, looking worriedly at Clare. Neither of them liked the idea of the nineteen-year-old Alison, who was always treated as the baby of the family, being so far away. "Doesn't she get some leave, now the exams are all over?"

"Yes, actually she says she'd like to spend it with me," Clare replied. "That means that she wants to unload about Keith and the trouble, whatever it was," she went on. "I know how squashed you are for space here, Sue, but would it be an awful nuisance if Alison shared my room? I wouldn't mind packing in. I'd feel better if she were here than at a hotel."

"Don't be silly, Clare. Of course she can come here. Hotel indeed—whatever would Tony say? Telephone her and tell her to come. Go on—do it now—she'll be wondering what on earth has been happening, waiting a week for an answer to a letter like that one!"

Clare needed no more urging. She got up and dialled her London number and waited.

Susan stirred her tea thoughtfully.

"Wonder what she looks like these days? D'you realise it's three years since I saw her? A rather plump kid of sixteen. Just before Mellie was born. Gosh, I remember that day so well. Alison took Jayne off my hands for a whole day."

She sipped her tea smiling a little at the memory, while Clare talked into the receiver. She had got the children's hospital at last and was waiting to be put through to the Nurses' Home.

"She was good with children even then," Clare agreed, still waiting.

"*Good!* That was the understatement of the year! Do you remember what a little tyrant Jayne was at eighteen months? You couldn't turn your back for one minute without she'd scuttle off and get into trouble. Remember the time she got treacle in her hair? Ugh! That was when I decided to have it cut short."

"That was a shame—you don't often see a babe of eighteen months with long curly hair," Clare said, severely, as she returned to the receiver. "Alison! Is that you? Your voice sounds all peculiar!"

Susan got up and took the cups out of the room. She was glad Clare had contacted Alison at last. They had all been rather anxious at the long silence.

Sounds of commotion came from above. Jayne fighting Mellie. Mellie bawling. Susan ran upstairs and hastily separated them. Jayne had managed to climb up to Mellie's cot and was hanging on. The chair she had climbed up on had been kicked away. Mellie was doing her best, between screams, to dislodge Jayne's clinging fingers from the cot rail. Jayne screamed too. Hers was a husky bellow compared to Mellie's shrill piercing efforts.

"Stop it, you two! Aunt Clare's on the telephone!" Susan scolded, picking Jayne off the cot with difficulty. "That wasn't very nice, was it? Who started it?"

13

Both the children firmly pointed to the other.

Susan sighed. "Well, in that case, I can't very well punish you both, can I? Come on, wash first and then tea. Let's see who can win, shall we?"

Mellie threw herself flat on her face in the cot and screamed that she didn't want a wash, didn't need a wash and wasn't going to have one. Susan took Jayne firmly by the hand and marched her to the bathroom.

It had started out as a pink bathroom, a symphony of shades from pale peach to old rose, with the acid touch of purple and black blossoms scuttering before an unseen wind. The curtains were pink and black towelling and, at one time, the towels and face flannels had echoed the colour scheme. Now it was a hotchpotch of miscellaneous coloured towels in varying states of age and repair, an odd assortment of toothbrushes in nursery holders, children's bath toys and drying underwear.

Susan wrinkled her nose in distaste. A small family was all very well but it did rather take the edge off things and leave pockets of dreariness like this bathroom.

By the time she had finished wrestling with Jayne and had got her moving downstairs towards tea there was a big puddle on the floor and a smashed toothmug to be cleared up. The children's mugs were of plastic, but this was Tony's mug that had got knocked down in the affray.

"I'm just not terribly good at being a mother, I suppose," she said to Clare who was now finished with the telephone. "Could you hang on to Jayne and keep her reasonably clean while I get the other brat ready?"

"OK. You go and see to Mellie. We'll be all right."

"Thanks. How's Alison?"

"Not too good. She had a cold and she's feeling very miserable," Clare said. "She cheered up though when I told her to come. Her holiday has actually started—yesterday—so I told her to come as soon as she liked. Was that okay?"

"It certainly was," Susan said, feelingly. "I might get the odd day off from these little horrors, if Alison's here all day."

She hurried to the door as there was the sound of a crash upstairs.

Clare took Jayne by the hand and sat her by her side on the settee.

"There was a little girl just like you at the doctor's today," she began. Jayne liked Clare's stories. They had got to the point where the girl at the doctor's had been changed into Jayne herself and was being taken to the Zoo by Alison when Susan came down with Mellie.

"She's knocked Tony's new bedside lamp down," Susan said, pulling a face. "I'll have to hide it for a while and hope he won't ask where it is. After the disappointment of me not being able to go with him—"

Her voice trailed away sadly as she hoisted Mellie up into her high chair.

"Don't tell Daddy, no, not never," Mellie said, earnestly.

"With a bit of luck we'll have Daddy on that plane for France and I might be able to get it mended before he comes back," Susan told her. She didn't want another session of screaming. "If only they could be trusted to share the same bedroom—it really is an awful nuisance having to have the cot in our room. Do you know, I've

16

had to take all the things off my dressing-table and put them up on a high shelf?"

Clare laughed. "Well, don't take on that disgusted tone when Alison arrives, or she'll be shocked from the start. I gather she's still as much in love with children as ever she was. Good thing; take her mind off Keith, perhaps."

"Ally coming?" Jayne asked, brightening. She didn't remember Alison, but Clare had often told her about the time when they were waiting for Mellie to arrive, and Alison had taken Jayne to London, to the Zoo. "Ally take Jayne to the Zoo?"

"Jayne Masters," said Susan, "you are rising five—just stop that baby talk this very minute."

Jayne's face crumpled.

"You don't like me, Mummy!" she stormed. "You hate me! Alison will like me—won't she, Clare?"

"Aunt Clare," Susan corrected, mechanically.

"Oh, I don't know—you can't expect them to call me Aunt Clare really," Clare objected. "I'm just their cousin and think what a lot of explaining you'll have to do when they're old enough to ask questions about it."

"I am," Susan said shortly. She shot out to the kitchen and came back wheeling the tea trolley. Underneath were plastic tray cloths, plastic feeders, a mopping up rag and unbreakable cups, plates and spoons for Jayne and Mellie. "I'm thinking, too, of Tony going to nice places where the food is served without mess, and there aren't any puddles to mop up. You don't know how nursery days can get one down, Clare."

"Don't I? I see the rough end of small fry in the surgery every morning," Clare retorted, laughing.

"Yes, the occasional child, and it's only there for a while and then it's the mother's responsibility. But when it's your own and you've got it all day and every day—"

She broke off to make a dive at the mug of milk, just saving it before Jayne managed to tip it over.

"See what I mean? Even when you get them to bed at night you can't just sit back and relax—things happen in the night too!"

"You know, you need this holiday as

18

much as Tony," Clare said, looking searchingly at her cousin. "You may not be as slick with children as Alison is but you like them well enough normally. I wonder if the doctor could cook up an idea to help? Would you like me to ask him?"

"Oh, I don't like worrying other people. Besides, it sounds so feeble. Please will someone take my kids off my hands so that I can go gallivanting abroad with my husband! Well, that's what people will say when it gets around," she remarked, vigorously tying Mellie's feeder behind her neck and catching a curl in the knot which produced a man-sized shriek from the little girl. "Sorry, lovey—didn't mean it," Sue said, retying the knot and giving Mellie a swift kiss, and coming away with jam on her face from Mellie's moist little mouth. "Oh, now look at me—typical Mum!"

"You go 'way with Daddy?" Jayne said, firmly.

"Yes, we got Clare," Mellie affirmed.

"You haven't, you know!" Clare said, laughing. "Poor Clare goes out to work every day. I can't take you two with me. That's a thought though, Sue, taking these two up to Wycherley Holt and letting them rip the study apart while Ewan Burnett tries to dictate his notes! Golly, that poor man would die. Can you imagine him with two young children around?"

It distracted Susan from her own problems for a few moments. "Frankly, no," she chuckled. "Still he'll be landed one of these days, I suppose. Some enterprising young woman will tot up what he's worth, and decide he's quite handsome in spite of being so stuffy, and make up her mind to take the plunge. Ever thought of it yourself, Clare?"

"Oh, goodness, no," Clare said, shuddering. "He is rather nice, I agree, but, to be honest, I like him best when his mind's on his work."

"Have you seen him when it isn't then?" Susan asked, amused, as she absently pushed fingers of jammy bread and butter into Mellie's receptive mouth.

"Um. Today. He really was rather odd. He didn't seem to want to work, which isn't like him. He talked the oddest nonsense, about me, and about Alison— well, I've told him a few things about her —had to, when he interviewed me. He wanted to know all about my family background."

"Yes, but why did he ask those things today, so specially?" Susan was interested to know.

"No idea. He talked about Dr. Shaw, too. I wish he wouldn't do that."

"You look so cross! Why?"

"Well, he isn't our patient, for a start. He goes up to London when he needs a consultation. But what put me out was that he asked me to go out and have a meal with him tonight."

"No!" Susan was almost incredulous. "Why didn't you say so before, Clare?" She looked at the clock. "Look at the time! You should have finished tea ages ago and started to get ready. What will you wear? You'll want a bath and the water isn't very hot!"

"Hold hard—I'm not going!" Clare protested.

"Not going! Why not?"

"Sue, I don't want to go out with him; not all that much, anyway. I put it off— said I'd got things to do. He looked a bit put out but I can't help it. I wasn't in the mood to go out with him tonight."

Susan considered her cousin. Clare, if she had given more time to dressing and grooming, would have been quite distinguished. She wished Clare would let her take her in hand. With those brown eyes, the fine bone structure of the eloquent face, and that dark hair, something could easily be done about her looks. There was a lot to work on and, come to think of it, Clare would make just the right sort of handsome, clever wife for a man like Ewan Burnett.

"Stop marrying me off to the man," Clare said, coolly. "I know what's going on in that head of yours. Drink that tea before it gets any colder. I'll cut up this piece of cake for Jayne."

"No, not yet. She hasn't had enough bread and butter—and don't be a beast, Clare. Why can't I get you all prettied up to go out with some nice man? Don't be too hasty about your boss. He's quite wealthy and there aren't so many nice men in this town, you know. Jayne, stop making that awful noise. You know you're not allowed cake before you've had enough bread and butter!"

"You go 'way with Daddy, Mummy!" Jayne stormed.

"I wish, sweetie, sometimes that I could," Susan said, grimly. "And if I could find someone to take charge of you all the time, I would, too."

"There's Alison," Jayne pointed out. "She likes me—Clare said so."

Susan's eyes met Clare's.

"I'm sorry, Sue, I was only telling her about how Alison took charge of her that day. Well, it kept her quiet while you were struggling with Mellie!"

"That's all right, Clare. I wasn't thinking about that. What I *was* thinking was that it's quite an idea, Alison having Jayne and Mellie if she's coming here to stay. Yes, it's quite an idea!"

2

THAT little suggestion which had come so oddly from the child was taken up and accepted with such alacrity that Clare wondered. But she knew that her cousin was badly in need of a holiday, although she hadn't quite realised how much both Susan and Tony needed to get away together, to find themselves again, as their manner now rather pointedly suggested.

Tony was so patently relieved at the idea of Alison coming to stay and taking over the responsibility of the children that he was almost boyish in his manner; a thing Clare had forgotten.

"Now wait a bit," she cautioned. "I daresay Alison will love the idea but don't let's rush our fences till we've had a chance to speak to her. You don't want to be disappointed if you find she can't do it."

"Why shouldn't she be able to do it?" he wanted to know.

"Well, she's had a bad shock—this row

with Keith. She only said she wanted to come and talk to me about it," Clare warned him. "She may not even want to stay here. After all, she's got a month's holiday due to her. She may decide to take off somewhere else, while she gets over it."

His disappointment and Susan's were so deep that Clare wished the matter had never been mentioned.

She hoped to be able to speak to Dr. Shaw about it the next morning in surgery but he was too busy to encourage private conversation.

There was a moment between patients when he did look receptively at her, as she was putting away some cards in the file, but before she could frame the words to ask him what he thought of the idea, he said quickly, "Well, did you go out last night, as I told you?"

"No, I didn't," she said, with a disarming smile. She had almost forgotten that instruction of his, as he had dropped her outside her cousin's house. "As a matter of fact there was a bit of a flap on at my cousin's so I stayed at home to talk it over."

His eyes flickered. He was interested. He was always ready and willing to listen to her problems. But the buzz of conversation just beyond the surgery door reminded them both that there was still a constantly filling waiting-room.

"Tell me about it after surgery," he said, and rang the bell for the next patient.

But they never got round to that conversation. He was called out urgently to the Sims' child.

She watched him go, her heart in her eyes. He drove himself too much and, as with Alison, children came first with him. He was so angry about that Sims' child.

Old Dr. Shaw came into the surgery.

"Where's my son?" he demanded.

She told him where Raymond Shaw had gone.

"Oh, the Sims," he commented, scowling. He looked sharply at her. "You working up at Burnett's, I hear?"

He was a gruff-voiced, tetchy caricature of the old-fashioned GP but she liked him.

"Yes," she agreed. "Dr. Raymond does know about it."

"H'm," he grunted, and seemed about to say a great deal more on the subject, but altered his mind. "How's your sister? My son tells me you've been worried about her. Nurse, isn't she?"

Clare was surprised that Raymond Shaw should have thought enough about the matter to repeat it to his father. She started talking to the old man and finally found herself sitting down companionably with him over a coffee and telling him all about the proposed trip abroad and how they were hoping that Alison might help out.

Old Dr. Shaw seemed to think it was a very good idea for a member of the family to come to Susan's rescue.

"Nice person, Susan," he commented quietly. "Don't know as I'd say the same about her husband but don't pass that on," he added, warningly.

"Why don't you like Tony, Dr. Shaw?"

"Didn't say I didn't like the fellow, did I? Just not so keen on him as Susan, but there—known Susan since she was a baby. Brought her into the world, in fact! Makes a difference. Husband was a newcomer to the town."

Clare had the impression that he almost said "foreigner" after the manner of all

Rexmundham people, who still cherished the lurking belief that Rexmundham was not only one of the oldest but the finest town in England.

He caught her half smile. "Ah, well, all very fine for you to look like that, young woman, but I also brought young Jayne into the world! Would have brought Mellie into the world, too, only I'd almost retired by then. She was brought into the world by my son."

He looked so fierce about it that Clare was reminded of what her cousin had said when she had first come to stay at their house. There had been trouble over both those babies. She tried to remember what it was, but all she could think of was strong opposition at the time of Mellie's birth, because the doctor wanted one thing and Tony had wanted another. What had it been?

She wracked her brains, not listening to the old doctor rambling on. Something to do with Tony wanting Susan to go up to London to the same nursing-home that his mother's friend was recommending so heartily.

Susan hadn't wanted to go. She wanted

the Shaws to attend her. This was her home (she was a Rexmundham girl so, of course, where else could be as good!) and Tony was a Londoner and impatient of provincial town feeling, impatient of the attendance of local GPs, impatient of all the stories he had heard of the Shaws and Susan's girlhood here.

There had been a row over that, Clare recalled, but she herself had been out of it, because of taking Jayne back to London with her, and she and Alison having the child for a whole fortnight, till Susan was able to think of coping.

The telephone rang, breaking into the reminiscences. Dr. Shaw dragged himself to his feet.

"Tell Susan to get away for a spell. Tell her I said so, even if it does mean traipsing over Europe with that hare-brained husband of hers. You can tell her I said that, too!" he growled, stumping out to take the phone call.

Clare didn't have a chance of telling Susan anything about it, however.

This was one of those elusive days when people were too busy or just not there. Raymond Shaw was too busy to stay and talk to her, and now Susan was out with the children for the day and only a note left on the hall table to say that her lunch would be ready in the automatic cooker and that she was to help herself.

In a way, Clare was glad to be going up to Ewan Burnett to work for the afternoon. Because Susan wasn't there to gossip Clare had more than enough time to walk all the way.

The way led through the town. Rexmundham on a fine Spring day was a gem of a town. In the main square the tall white houses sat sedately round a cobbled circle in which stood the Memorial.

The Town Hall, the Museum and Public Library, were all architecturally in keeping. The shops still had the Georgian frontage to the High Street, though new extensions had been added but cleverly and decently hidden and approached through arcades which were closed at night behind iron grilles. Even the cinema was in a converted building that still kept the same aloof and architecturally correct frontage.

But Clare had grown used to the town and preferred it to London. She did some shopping, but forgot the Postal Orders Sue had asked her for. She went back into the Post Office. Miss West, behind the telegraphs grille, called to her.

"I didn't think I'd be seeing you, dear. We tried to deliver this telegram to your cousin's house but there's been no one there all the morning. It's for you."

The telegram was from Alison. She was coming on the down train and would arrive that evening.

That raised a problem. Clare didn't think that Susan had got the spare bed in her room ready yet. She hadn't looked at lunch-time. It still had its silk cover on, to match Clare's own. Oh, well, that could be attended to later. Meantime, she had better telephone Susan when she was ready to leave Ewan Burnett's house to tell her that she would be going to the station, to pick up Alison on the way home.

Ewan Burnett lived in the old manor house known locally as Wycherley Holt. It was a gracious house, ivy-covered, crouching comfortably in its framework of fine old trees, but inside the house all was clean and modern.

Ewan had literally stripped the inside

and filled it with lovely things, when he had first come here. It was a large home for a bachelor and aroused a great deal of speculation locally at first, until the district regretfully decided that his guests were all likely to remain literary folk. Still, the odd matchmaking local mother had a try occasionally, with a pretty daughter, since it was well known that Ewan didn't depend entirely on his writing for a living. He had inherited money.

Clare found him already sitting at his desk in the tall, beautifully proportioned library. But the paper inserted in his machine was blank.

Ewan Burnett seemed disinclined to work for once.

"Sit down at my desk, Clare. I've one or two things I want to discuss with you," he began. But, after pacing the room for a while he said it could wait.

He showed her some photographs of his travels instead, and tried to draw her out on how she had lived and worked before she had come to him.

She told him frankly about her typing experience in London.

"But you know all that, Mr. Burnett,"

she said, just a little puzzled at the trend of his thoughts. "You've got all my details in your file."

"I was just refreshing my memory," he said slowly. "Clare, the last time I asked you you said you hadn't anyone special in your life. Is that still true?" he asked, quietly.

She looked at him a little doubtfully and a little surprised. In the months that she had worked for him he had always been the same. A tall, scholarly, distinguished looking man of about forty, with a thread of silver in dark brown hair; a carefully trimmed brown moustache, and reading glasses with an exaggerated shaped frame that added rather than detracted from his distinctive good looks. A quiet man, with a depth of concentration while he was working that never admitted this kind of odd, personal conversation. It was his impersonal manner that had appealed to her so much and this was the second time it had vanished. She was uneasy.

"No, there's no one special in my life, Mr. Burnett," she replied in a level tone.

"So that your evenings are mainly free?"

"Yes, but—" she began.

"It's a job I'm asking you to do," he said, quickly, looking as awkward as Clare was feeling.

"Oh, I didn't realise. Well, I'd be glad to help you, if I'm not baby-sitting or helping Dr. Shaw," she said with a sincerity that robbed the words of any unhappy meaning. "Would it be every evening—and, if so, how long—?"

"No," he cut in, "just the odd occasion only."

"Then that's all right. What would the work be? Typing?"

He shook his head.

"I'm afraid I'm rather a long time coming to the point," he remarked. "As a matter of fact, it's a little embarrassing. You remember that I did suggest that we might have dinner together. I thought it might be easier that way, but you didn't appear to be able to get free that evening. Now I feel that perhaps you'd prefer to discuss it here in this more formal atmosphere."

She remembered that suggestion of his only too well. So he hadn't just been asking her out to dinner from mere social reasons! How Susan would fume when she realised that her match-making ideas were all for nothing, Clare thought in amusement.

"If it's a job, Mr. Burnett, I think it might be better to discuss it here," Clare agreed, with a smile that may have meant relief.

"Well, the fact is, an old friend of mine has a daughter. A pretty young daughter with romantic ideas. She thinks she would like to be engaged to a successful writer and she has already shown signs of the most disturbing intentions where I am concerned."

He half-smiled and eased his collar.

"Needless to say," he went on, after a slight pause, "I find it more distressing than I can say. I am only too well aware of my own inadequacy when it comes to this sort of thing. Now, I wondered if you would be so kind as to step into the breach and accompany me to those social functions where I am likely to run into my old friend and her daughter. It would be much kinder this way than to have to tell the child that I don't want to be bothered by her infatuation."

"But I'm not quite clear about the plan.

Will it work? I mean, how can your part-time secretary—"

"Oh, dear, Clare, I don't seem to have explained myself very well, do I? What I hoped was to spread the idea that we—you and I—have an understanding. Not a definite engagement. I wouldn't suggest such a thing to you—but just an understanding. If you have no one special so that this idea might cause harm, then surely—? What do you think?"

He felt uncomfortable beneath her cool, surprised look.

"It would be deceitful, wouldn't it?" she said, unequivocally. "Your friends won't like it when they find out the truth."

"I don't see how they *could* find out," he said. "After all, it would be quite secret between us and, besides, people with an understanding between them can always have second thoughts later."

That, she had to admit, was true enough about having second thoughts. But she did not believe that it could be kept secret. If she were seen about with Ewan Burnett everyone would inevitably know about it and draw their conclusions. There would be gossip columns in the local press. Ewan

Burnett was no mere nonentity. He was, of course, only too well aware of that and was, no doubt, relying on it to help his plan.

But what would that do for Clare's future life?

She thought of her secret dreams about Raymond Shaw. What would he think? Not that she had any need to worry about his thoughts on the subject. As she had told Susan, so far as Raymond Shaw was concerned, she was just part of the fixtures and fittings.

But, one day, might it not be different if she didn't get her name coupled with anyone else's?

She wrestled briefly with herself but she couldn't bring herself to do this job for Ewan Burnett.

He stood watching her narrowly.

"Don't make a decision now, Clare. It's an outrageous idea, I realise, now I've put it into words. Very feeble of me, too, to be forced to ask for your help. But, to be frank, that young lady can just make rings round me with her charm and her modern outlook. She terrifies me. Do think it over

—there are two whole weeks before I need see them again. Help me—will you?"

She nodded dumbly but she knew that her answer would ultimately be the same. While she dreamed of appearing one day to Raymond Shaw as a girl and not merely his secretary, then she'd hang on and hope and, meantime, she had no intention of getting publicly entangled with Ewan Burnett or anyone else.

3

ALISON alighted from the train and had almost walked the length of the platform towards her sister before Clare realised she was there.

"Alison, darling, I didn't recognise you!" Clare cried, giving her an affectionate hug. "Let me look at you. What have you done to yourself?"

She held her sister off and took in the details of a very smart little London suit, fur-edged at the throat, with a fur-trimmed hat to match, and very smart high-heeled shoes. The last time she had seen Alison in mufti, it had been a teen-age sweater, trews and flat sandals.

"I've grown up," Alison said, quietly. "Oh, but it's good to see you, Clare!" and she hugged her sister, partly from pleasure at the reunion, partly to hide the suspicious wobble in her voice. She hadn't grown up all that much.

"What have you done to your hair? Where's your luggage? Let's get that settled, then we can find a cab—or would you prefer to go and eat somewhere and talk?"

"Eat and talk," Alison said, promptly, so Clare went to find Willy Tunks.

"He comes to collect stuff off this train and he has to pass Sue's street—oh, there he is. Wait a jiff. No, come and make his acquaintance—he's a useful customer. Then we'll go to the new tea-rooms that have opened behind the High Street. Miss Odstock's Parlour. Don't laugh—actually it's rather nice, and all home-made food. She keeps open until ten thirty, too, which is a real boon in Rexmundham!"

After they had settled about the luggage they walked down from the station. Alison looked at everything and everyone as if she were really on holiday, and not as if her heart was breaking over Keith, her beloved Keith.

They found a corner table in Miss Odstock's, because they were early.

"We can talk here all right. It's not likely to fill up yet," Clare said, and gave her attention to ordering.

"Now, then, that's settled! Let's have a look at you, Alison, my sweet. Oh, a very nice London hair-cut. You won't get a layer cut like that in Rexmundham, I'm afraid."

"Well, honey, I'm not likely to need one, am I? I'm only here for a short stay," Alison said.

"But for the whole month, surely?" Clare was moved to protest.

"You've got plans made for me," Alison replied, trying to smile.

In spite of the skilful make-up and the new hair-do Alison hadn't changed a great deal, Clare now saw. Her sister hadn't any good looks at all, really. Just even features, an open, rather young face, and wide hazel eyes. But her smile transformed her. That smile and the blazing sincerity, and the utter restfulness about her, were Alison's main features. But apparently they weren't enough to keep Keith Everton inter-ested . . .

"Only for the month," Clare said, firmly. "That is, unless you've got plans already made. Have you?"

"If you mean plans that include Keith Everton, no, I haven't, so you'd better tell me what your plans are for me, Clare."

"All right, sweetie." The food came

and, when it had been served, Clare said, "Remember Susan's two infants—Jayne and Mellie?"

There it was, the blazing smile as Alison remembered Jayne at the Zoo that day.

"Mellie was only a baby when I saw her. What's she like now? Still tiny and a bit of a kitten?"

"No, indeed not!" Clare said almost choking, and then launching into a drily humorous account of their latest exploits.

"How comes no one ever sent me photographs of them?" Alison said, laughing herself as Clare finished.

"First catch your brat and keep it still long enough for a picture to be taken," Clare said, as though it were well nigh impossible. "Oh, there have been some snaps but they weren't all that good, for the same reason. Does it interest you, the idea of taking them on for a bit to help Susan?"

"Taking them on? Oh, yes, I'd love to, while I'm staying here, you mean? That means Sue can put me up?"

"I'm telling this awfully badly, I'm afraid," Clare admitted, and launched into a rather more careful and certainly not hilarious account of how Jayne set the idea in motion of having Alison take charge of them both in their parents' absence.

"Alison, I rather rashly said that I thought it would be right up your street, but you can back out if you want to. I know you adore kids, especially young Jayne, although, of course, you've lost touch. I know you always liked Sue and, although people don't go for Tony so much, I personally like him and I'd like to help them both."

Alison made patterns on the tablecloth with a clean fork, apparently lost in thought.

"It would be an awful responsibility for someone like me, who doesn't really understand kids, but I thought you might take it in your stride, what with your training, and your flair for making the little brutes do as you want them to. At least, you used to have it—have you still got it?"

"Oh, yes, I can persuade *children* to do as I want them to," Alison said, quietly but with an edge to her voice that had never been there before.

"It's a way out for you, as regards somewhere to live, because to be honest I don't know where I'd begin to look for digs or a hotel in this place," Clare went on. "I did suggest a hotel to Sue, but it was a gesture—I hadn't much real hope, they all seem to fill up so quickly—but, of course, Sue said what an idea and cried me down. And then this idea came up. You know how ideas crop up and it seems so important for them to get away together. It's supposed to be because Tony's boss wants Sue to go—but frankly, I've got the uneasy feeling that there's more to this, this need for getting away, than the boss or the chance of foreign travel and a holiday."

"What do you mean?" Alison asked, quietly.

"I don't quite know how to put it, and you must keep it under your hat, Alison, but I get the odd feeling that if Susan and Tony don't get away together soon, just to be by themselves, I don't know—I'm not sure—but I think their marriage might begin to crack."

"Why?" Alison asked, bluntly.

"I don't know exactly. Just drifting

apart, I suppose—two nice people forced apart by circumstances, kids—honestly, they are a handful, those two, and Sue hasn't got your gift for coping with small fry. But of course, it's just my own feeling —except—(come to think of it) that rather odd remark Dr. Shaw made this morning. Something about 'if she could manage to get away now, he'd feel happier, for one'. Of course he couldn't know—or could he? The Shaws have looked after Sue's family for ages. He told me this morning that he brought Sue into the world."

"Sue's marriage likely to crack up," Alison repeated. Her food was now cold, but she didn't seem to notice, as she took up her fork again and began to eat. "Well, in that case, I'll do it. Yes, that's settled, just because of *that*, Clare!"

"Oh, darling, I'm so glad!" Clare said, warmly, but she took a close look at Alison. "What pushed you to make up your mind? Similar circumstances—or don't you want to discuss it?"

"You know me," Alison said, her lips wobbling again, "always running to you with my woes. I'll tell you, as you've asked me. Keith and I had a row over a girl—a medical student. She's pretty and he's good-looking and he wouldn't tell me why she had been in his car with him. Well, my point of view is, if you can't trust the other person then it isn't any use going on."

"Now look, honey—" Clare began, in surprised protest at this sweeping assertion.

"Is there anyone special in your life?" Alison thrust suddenly at her sister.

Clare's eyes dropped. "I'm a bit silly over someone who doesn't realise I'm alive, if that answers your question," she said, at last.

"Oh! Sorry. Didn't mean to probe, Clare, but, what I really mean is, unless you've been in love, you can't say what's sensible or not. You can't really know what it's all about. Believe me, it's plain hell. More suffering to it than nice patches. Anyway, I ought to have known."

"What d'you mean—you ought to have known? You don't mean that Keith was flirtatious?"

"No, of course not! Nothing like that. But frankly, I have got eyes in my head, haven't I? I'm not a raving beauty, and that girl was just that! Well, it stands to reason which one he'd prefer."

"But my dear stupid little kid sister, a man doesn't, if he's worth the candle, go for looks alone!" Clare protested.

"No, but it helps," Alison retorted.

They walked home after they had finished their meal. Susan was back, embroiled in the hectic business of getting the children to bed. Alison's luggage had arrived and was piled precariously in the little hall.

Susan greeted Alison with delight.

"I'm more glad you've come at last than I can say," she told Alison. "Ever since we heard you were to arrive today these children have been impossible. Look at them now!"

Mellie had scrambled out of her cot somehow and had staggered to the top of the stairs, trailing a blanket over one shoulder. Jayne had got out of her bath and was hopping about, naked and wet, beside her sister on the landing.

"Jayne, back into the bathroom at once!" Susan shouted, prepared to storm up the stairs.

"Let me go," Alison said, quietly. "Might as well make their acquaintance."

She peeled off the fur-trimmed jacket as she went, and handed it absently over her shoulder. It was Clare who took it from her. The little hat went the same way and she kicked off the high-heeled shoes before she reached the top of the stairs.

Alison hadn't changed much after all, Clare thought, with swift relief. This was how she had always been; casual over clothes and appearance when it came to the rival attraction of children.

She cuddled and kissed them both, talking at top rate. Their voices intermingled joyously, and Susan felt curiously shut out as she watched Alison scoop up a child under each arm and go off to the bathroom.

Squeals of delight and splashings came from that room while Clare helped Susan to make up the second bed for Alison. Whatever else happened tonight, certainly Mellie and Jayne were enjoying the bath for once.

"I do believe she's got Mellie back in the bath again with Jayne!" Susan said, getting to her feet after tucking the bottom sheet in.

Clare put a hand on her cousin's arm.

"Oh, let it go. What's it matter for once? They'll sleep like tops, those two!"

"Yes, but what about when we come back from our holiday? They'll be spoilt with all this but they won't get fun in the bath from me," Susan grumbled.

"Never mind, sufficient to the day!" Clare grinned. "Come on, I bet you haven't had anything to eat. I'll help you get a meal for Tony and yourself. We've had ours."

Susan looked sharply at Clare.

Clare explained hastily, "I thought it might give me a chance to talk to Alison before she met all of you. She looked a bit weepy. It did give her a chance to settle in, and she has said she'd be very glad to take the job on for the whole month, so you've nothing to worry about."

"Oh, good," Susan said, briefly. "Well, I don't think I'll bother to eat, myself. Tony won't be home till late. He phoned to say he was having a bite in the office. He's staying on to clear up some work—him and that secretary of his."

So that was it, Clare thought wryly. "Then we'll make a quick snack and have it with you. You've got to eat something," she said, deliberately ignoring what her cousin had just said. In Susan's present state she would be suspicious of anything or anyone.

She hoped that Alison's presence would make that much difference so that Susan and Tony could come to terms with each other before they went away for this much-needed holiday.

Alison's presence in the house made an unbelievable difference. From that evening onwards the children—if not being less mischievous—were certainly happier. It was as if Alison was able to fulfil a need for them. She had a radiant personality with children. Shouts of laughter, first thing next morning, from Jayne's room, reminded Clare of this.

Usually there was a storm of weeping, shouts and temper, for Jayne wasn't the sunniest soul early in the morning. Alison changed all that. From the first morning it was fun getting up and dressing. Alison's nursing training had ingrained early rising so everyone had an early morning cup of tea; a thing that normally happened only at week-ends.

"Oh, Alison, aren't I glad you came?" Clare said, as her sister sailed in next morning with tea for both of them and bowls of cornflakes. "Sue's a dear, but I'm usually glad to get out of here in the morning."

"This is good for me, too," Alison said, quietly. "I had the choice of moping in the Nurses' Home or moping at some small hotel where I was supposed to be getting sea air and a rest. I shan't have time for moping here!"

Alison had discarded her brief grooming and glamour. She had on a short sleeved sweater this morning, and stretch pants. Her hair was hidden in a chiffon scarf and, after a brief chat with Clare, she rushed to take the children out of their parents' room and down to breakfast. Alison's idea of nursery breakfast had an odour that brought the adults down, too. Susan's burnt toast and over-fried eggs never invited anyone.

"Why didn't we discover you before, Alison?" Tony said, thoughtfully, as he got up to go. "This has been one of the most pleasant breakfast times we've had for a long while."

He caught Susan's eye. Susan was usually behind time, not exactly good-tempered, head-achy and bothered by the children, first thing, so he hastily amended it to: "The kids are a perfect delight with a visitor in the house—you must come more often."

The awkward moment passed but Clare was glad when they had scattered; Tony to the station, Susan to the hairdresser's and she herself on the way to the surgery.

Raymond Shaw was already there, and they had ten minutes before surgery opened, so he said, "Oh, good, you're early, Clare—how about telling me what was on your mind yesterday?"

She talked to him while she was getting out notes of some of the patients they expected that morning. Most of what she had told his father yesterday, with the added news that Alison had arrived, and disarmed everyone.

It was odd how interested he was in Alison.

"Has she really broken it off with this chap Everton?" he wanted to know.

"It looks like it," Clare sighed. "She's got this bee in her bonnet about being plain (she isn't really—at least, I don't think so) and the other girl is so pretty, and I can't make her see that it doesn't always count."

"It might, with Everton," Raymond Shaw said, with perception rather than acidity.

She looked sharply at him. He was really terribly good-looking. Not in the distinguished way that Ewan Burnett was handsome, but in a rugged style that reminded her of a sculptured head before the sculptor has fined off the features. She was furious with herself for caring so much, angry at the sick longing that rose in her when she was alone with him.

"Would good looks count with you?" she couldn't stop herself from asking.

"Oh, yes, indeed," he said. "It's a pleasant fiction that a chap doesn't want a good-looking wife if she has other virtues, but I don't think it weighs really. Every man wants to feel that his wife is prettier than the next chap's. I'm sure your sister can't be all that plain. When are *we* going to meet her?"

She turned away.

"Probably this morning. Jayne's leg needs looking at and I gather that my cousin would feel happier if she knew before she went away that there was no infection. I said they could walk round this morning, but not to bother you if they found the waiting-room full."

"Send them in to see me no matter what it's like out there," he said. "I'd like another look at young Jayne's leg. When is your cousin going away, did you say?"

She didn't answer him at once. She had caught sight of herself in the mirror over the desk. Scrubbed clean and efficient in her white coat, her hair caught back in a slick, neat, sensible style. So he liked them pretty, did he, she jeered at herself? What chance did she think she herself would stand with him, ever?

"What's the matter, Clare?" he asked, sharply.

"Sorry. I was thinking. What were you saying?" she said, flushing a little.

She prayed that her thoughts wouldn't show in her face. It was sickening to be like this over the man you worked for. She played with the idea of saying yes, after all, to Ewan Burnett's proposal. At least it would show herself that she possessed a decent amount of pride.

He repeated his question but she was saved from answering him by the slamming of the waiting-room door, and the chiming clock in the hall reminded them it was opening time for the surgery.

When Alison called with the children, she was windblown, her cheeks flushed and pink, her eyes bright.

Raymond Shaw was clearly impressed. He shook her hand warmly and questioned her about her work and her hospital while he looked at Jayne's knee.

"What are you going to do with yourself all day long with these brats?" he asked Alison at length, when he had finished with Jayne and found a jar of pieces of cut chocolate for both of them.

"Well, this afternoon I thought I'd take them to get their photographs done. Quick ones, so they're ready for my cousin and her husband to take away with them. I know my sister says they don't keep still long enough, but I can manage them, I think," Alison said, with simple and easy confidence.

He watched that dazzling smile which she turned on to the children, as if he couldn't tear his eyes away.

"That's in the High Street?" he enquired more as a statement than a question.

"Oh, yes, but it won't take long, so I thought I'd walk them to the quarry for a picnic tea. Then we could come back to meet my sister on her way home from Wycherley Holt."

"You'll never do it, with the children," he said, definitely. "I'll pick you up at the quarry and give you a lift to Burnett's place to pick up Clare. It's all on my way —with a bit of luck I might have finished rounds by then."

"That would be very kind of you, Dr. Shaw," Alison said, warmly. "I'm sure my cousin Susan would want you to drop in for some tea after bringing us all home."

"I'd be glad to," he replied, with equal charm.

Clare was flabbergasted. Alison was certainly getting VIP treatment! Usually Dr. Shaw avoided young women.

He showed Alison and the children out

through the hall and, on the way, she heard them meeting his father. Then the front door slammed and Raymond came back.

"Well, Clare, you were justified in the build-up you gave that sister of yours. She's all you led us to expect. My father says so, too. She has the most dazzling smile I have ever seen. And don't those youngsters adore her? But she's not plain, Clare. Don't let her think she is."

At that moment Clare felt that she really didn't know him. He was the last person to get excited over a girl, she felt, especially at such short notice.

And yet, when the patients started coming in again and she slipped back into the familiar routine—taking telephone calls, holding a child here for him to dress a wound, hushing a squawling baby there while the doctor examined the young mother—Clare felt as if Alison's visit to the surgery had been a dream. He made no further reference to Alison and, when he was called out to a local emergency, he was his old preoccupied self.

Susan was back again, and whipping up one of her surprise lunches when Clare got home. She seemed pleased that the doctor was giving them all a lift, but clearly her mind was so filled with the coming trip abroad, that she attached no special significance to the incident. Clare was glad she said nothing, for Alison didn't yet know that the doctor was the man Clare had referred to the evening before, when Alison had asked her if she was in love.

She left Alison preparing for their picnic. Susan had a hundred things to do to get herself and Tony ready for their travelling. She was rushing around with a list of things to buy, things to have cleaned, and things Tony wanted seen to and hadn't had time to attend to himself. Before he went he had to go to London and stay the night. Susan had received this news with tight lips and hadn't waited to hear the reason from Tony.

Ewan Burnett looked keenly at Clare when she arrived.

"Something's wrong," he said.

Clare denied it. "Why do you say that?" she asked.

"You look tired, strained. How about

taking the afternoon off? I can manage making more notes."

One half of her wanted badly to be free of him today. He would be sure to raise again the question of that scheme of his and she wasn't ready even to think about it. On the other hand, the doctor had already arranged to collect Alison and the children and to call for her.

She shook her head. "No, it's kind of you but I'd rather not. It will only pile work up. My sister has arrived, so things should be easier."

And he, of course, wanted to hear about Alison but not with quite the same interest as Raymond Shaw had shown. He was far more preoccupied with his coming visit to Bodcarne Castle for some research on an old battle.

"Clare, now that your sister has come will that give you more freedom, or less?" he asked, breaking off in his dictation a little while later.

"For what? You mean to come and do extra work for you?" Clare asked cautiously.

"No, I was thinking how much easier it would be if you went with me to the castle and took my notes for me on the spot. It would make a break for you, if you're not doing anything else. Think about it, will you?"

However he said no more about it and when she left that afternoon she had already forgotten it.

Alison and the children were full of the picnic they had had, and Raymond Shaw sat quietly at the wheel listening, chuckling occasionally. Relaxed, happier than she had seen him for a long time, and although his eyes were glued to the road ahead in his usual careful way of driving, he was very much with them as a party, his former remoteness gone.

"We had choc ices," Mellie said, ecstatically. "Doctor Shaw brought them."

"And he played Tag with us in the quarry," Jayne said, smugly, "and I let him find me, behind a bush."

Alison cuddled her, laughing, but Raymond Shaw said, with raised eyebrows, "That child needs watching—she has advanced ideas."

They talked so much—Alison and the children—that Clare had no need to do more than to put in the odd word. She felt curiously out of it. Alison and the children had been sitting by the doctor on the broad front seat. Clare had gone in the back when they had picked her up. This, too, added to the illusion of her being far removed from him. And when he did say something, it seemed to be directed at Alison and not Clare.

Oh, heavens, I'm not liking it when I ought to be glad for Alison's sake, she told herself. But she wasn't glad, and she couldn't whip up the smallest bit of comfort in the thought that this was just what Alison needed, to help her get over her estrangement with Keith Everton.

I'm mean-minded, she told herself, disgustedly, but she couldn't do a thing about it. This was the way she had dreamed of being picked up by the doctor, only, when it had happened before, he had seemed so remote, his humour forced, and his mind taken up with his patients. She might have been any stranger to whom he was giving a lift. She had wanted so badly to have him look like that at her, smile like that at her, hang on her words, as he seemed to hang on Alison's.

This time he didn't just stop at the end

of Susan's road; he went right up to her house.

"Your cousin is going away on Saturday, yes?" he asked, but it was a question divided between Alison and Clare so she left her sister to answer it.

"Well, you'll be at a loose end on Sunday, I imagine," he went on, "so what about a day out? It's time I had a bit of a break myself."

Alison looked at Clare and back at him.

"It would be wonderful," she said, "but what about the morning rounds and being back in time for evening surgery?"

"My father will take both, for once," Raymond Shaw told her, with a cheerful grin. "I shall play truant."

"Would you mind if we went, Clare?" Alison asked, clearly under the impression that Clare wasn't included in the party.

"Clare's coming too, aren't you?" the doctor said, in surprise. "Or are you doing something else?"

"No, I'm not doing anything else, but are you sure you want me to come? Alison can manage the children without my help."

"Oh, no, come too, Clare," but it was

Alison who begged her to go with them. Not the doctor. He just sat very quietly, watching her, as if trying to read her thoughts.

4

THE Saturday that Susan and Tony departed was a curious day. Alison and the children, with Clare, went to the local station to see them off, and Clare went on to morning surgery.

Alison made the morning interesting for Mellie and Jayne by taking them to the local store to be fitted for new shoes, and then there was the toy department, the restaurant for ice-cream, and the ceremonial taking of bread to the park to feed the ducks. She had planned a cold salad for lunch, and there was a flan in the fridge waiting to be filled with fruit and cream.

Alison had the talent of making the most ordinary shopping an adventure, and every street they went down seemed to remind her of a similar street in her own childhood where something exciting had happened. Alison's childhood had been dull in the extreme but, to hear her talk, the spellbound Mellie and Jayne would never have known any better.

This morning, however, something nagged at Jayne. She wasn't quite five and often seemed as babyish as the three-year-old Mellie, but today she had guilt on her conscience.

"Are Mummy and Daddy coming back some day?" she suddenly demanded.

"Silly Jayne, of course they are!" Alison said, recovering quickly from her shock in time to smile reassuringly down at the child.

"No, they're not. Not never!" Jayne averred.

"Want Mummy and Daddy!" Mellie said, loudly.

Alison thought quickly. "I've got something to show you both, so you'll know just when Mummy and Daddy will be coming back," and she found a seat where the ducks were still in view, in case the new game should pall.

She had bought them exercise books half an hour before. She borrowed one to rule up the month.

"Now, this first square is today—a sort of magic today because it's only little. That's the day they went on a train and an aeroplane. Now, every day we'll block it out in a different colour, and you can take it in turns to do it. And by the time we get to number 31, that's the day they'll be coming home."

"That's a long way away," Jayne spluttered, a big tear splashing down her cheek.

"Oh, is it?" Alison asked, innocently. "I thought it would be a gorgeous lot of days to do lovely things and have an exciting time ourselves, before they come back. And they'll want to know what we've been doing, so I thought we might keep a diary—you know, writing down what we do each day, so we can show them."

"How?" Mellie asked stolidly. Anything with the words "exciting" and "holiday" in appealed to her strongly.

"Never mind how," Jayne said. "They've gone and they're not coming back, not never, because I said I didn't want them to come back! I said it!"

Mellie started to cry in earnest. Alison thoughtfully popped a piece of chocolate in her mouth and turned to Jayne.

"Now, don't you think you'd better explain what all that's about, Jayne, because I haven't an idea what you're talking about. I happen to know where they're going to be each day and I happen to know they've booked seats on the plane to come back at the end of this month. What do you think now?"

"Mummy was cross with me and I said I hoped she'd go away and never come back, not never," Jayne stated, with such an effort that Alison was near tears herself for the child.

"Well, that was just being naughty, but I don't suppose your Mummy would take any notice of that. She likes her home and she'd want to come back with Daddy, now wouldn't she?"

"I said I hoped they wouldn't never come back, not her nor Daddy," Jayne maintained fiercely, with a curious pleasure in the thought of her badness.

"That won't make any difference to their plans but I hope you said you were sorry, Jayne," Alison told her firmly.

"No, I couldn't, because they were talking about Clare's blind man," Jayne gasped. "I wanted to say I was sorry; I wanted to!"

"Well, I'm sure it will be all right. I tell

you what—how would it be to write a letter to Mummy and say sorry, then you won't have to worry about it the whole gorgeous holiday, will you?" she suggested, cuddling Jayne.

"Yes! That's a *thuper* idea," Mellie shouted. "Me write sorry, too!"

"You can't even write!" Jayne said, scornfully.

"But she can put kisses and that's just as good," Alison said, encouragingly. "Kisses with coloured crayons—each one a different colour. How about that?"

"Yes, and I want to say sorry in different colours," Jayne urged, anxiously. "That'd make it look nicer, wouldn't it?"

"That would be lovely," Alison agreed. "But what's this about Clare's blind man? Are you sure you got that right?"

"Of course I am! What paper shall I write sorry on?" the practical Jayne demanded.

"When we get home I'll sort out some pretty paper for both of you. Now what about Clare?"

"Oh, they were just talking about some man and Mummy wanted her to marry him and Clare said he couldn't ever see her so that means he's blind," Jayne said, patiently, as if she were talking to a half-wit. "Now, can we go home and write that letter?"

Alison got up and turned towards home, her thoughts churning about. Was this the man that Clare had said she was silly over? The one who wasn't even aware that she was alive?

Alison suddenly thought she knew what the child had overheard and she laughed aloud.

"Did Clare say he *couldn't* see her or that he *didn't* see her?" she asked carefully, holding Jayne still to look at her.

"Same thing," Jayne said, cheerfully.

"No, darling, not the same thing at all. But you're too little to know that!"

"I'm not! I'm nearly five and I can read, can't I?" Jayne stormed, kicking out to free herself.

Alison held her legs down. "No, that's not nice, darling," she said firmly, and Mellie was flabbergasted to see her sister stop kicking and fling her arms round Alison's neck. "I wasn't kicking you, I was just kicking!" Jayne said, contritely.

"That's all right, sweetie," Alison comforted her. "I understand. And you're a very clever girl of rising five and I know you are going to be very bright at school and get to the top of your class, but there's one thing we have to be very careful about, and that's not to say a thing until we're sure about it. Now did Clare say this poor man *couldn't* see her, or *didn't?* It is very important, darling."

"Don't know," Jayne said, sullenly, because now that it had been put like that to her, she honestly couldn't remember. She hadn't really been listening. She had been thinking stormily that her mother was always on at her, and not so much at Mellie, although to Jayne's way of thinking Mellie was just as naughty in a different way.

"Oh. Oh, well, never mind, you did try," Alison said. But her disappointed tones cut Jayne who felt she had let down the person she was so fond of.

"She said she thought she was furniture," Jayne said, and added, "she works for him."

"She works for him!" Alison echoed, blankly. "Thinks she's the furniture!"

"Yes. She said, 'he doesn't see me, I might as well be the furniture'," Jayne said, smugly aware that many people had said before now in her hearing that she had a photographic memory and that that was something special. "And his name's a funny one."

Alison walked along quietly, thinking over this surprising piece of news. Should she ask Clare about it, or should she wait for confidences? Funny, she had thought that there was something boiling up between Clare and the doctor. She had had a sort of feeling that there was a certain tension between them, but perhaps that wasn't love. It might be that they didn't get on well, working together, and that Clare had got this other employer, to gradually make the switch. It was all very unsettling, because she had looked on her sister as one of the solid kind who managed their lives with efficiency and tidiness and now it appeared that Clare's love life was in as much of a mess as her own!

"It's Burnett," Mellie put in, having eaten the rest of the chocolate and felt that attention should be turned to herself. "I know, 'cos Mummy said so. Mishter Burnett and he writes story books."

"Oh, she doesn't know!" Jayne said, scornfully. "But I do—I've just remembered what his name is—it's Ewan Burnett and Daddy says he's a pompous ass. I heard him."

That did it. Alison smoothly turned the conversation into the less dangerous topic of selecting notepaper to write the "sorry" letter to Mummy and Daddy.

When Clare came home that day she looked ruffled. Alison said softly, "I wonder if a GP is less tractable than the kind we have on the wards? You look as if you've got that week-end feeling!"

"Oh, it's nothing, Alison, only—well we've got a patient who upsets him."

"Who's him? Old or young Dr. Shaw?"

"Both, actually," Clare evaded. "The parents of a very delicate child, and they obstruct in the belief that they are madly helpful."

"It's a worrying job you've got at the surgery," Alison said, thoughtfully. "In a way, it's a good thing your other job's so different. You enjoy working for Mr Burnett, don't you?"

Clare looked sharply at her sister. "No more than at the surgery. What made you think that?"

This wasn't going to be easy, Alison saw.

"It was an idea I had," she said, carefully. "Never mind. What I was really thinking of was asking you exactly what your days and times were so that I can fix up to keep the children occupied every minute. A rather disturbing thing happened this morning," and briefly she told Clare about the children's distress regarding their parents' absence.

Clare was torn between frustration and amusement.

"Oh, that Jayne, she's an actress. She can turn on the tears at any minute! Don't let her take you in, Alison."

"You mean you don't think she really meant a word of it?"

"Of course not. At least, she probably started out putting on an act, and then scared herself so convincing was she about it. Listen, Alison, that child got a great deal of satisfaction out of telling poor Susan she'd be glad if her parents went away and dear Alison came from London

73

to look after them—and don't forget she hadn't seen you for three years and didn't remember you!"

Alison thought about it, and shook her head.

"You can say what you like, but that child is going to miss her mother. That's what I meant when I asked you about your times. When you're working I'm going to take them right away from the house, either for long walks or bus rides, but I'll pack food and get them to places they haven't been to before. Once they're used to being without Susan and Tony it will work out, I'm sure."

"Yes, it might work out very well," Clare admitted, slowly. "You see, Ewan Burnett wants me to go with him to Bodcarne Castle to take notes on the spot. I'd hedged a bit about going, because I didn't want to leave you alone too much with the children, but, if that's what you've got in mind, it might work out quite well."

"Then you do that," Alison said, warmly, reading more into Clare's bothered face than she should have.

This, then, was what young Jayne had

unwittingly touched on—this problem of Clare's love for an employer who couldn't see that she cared about him. Perhaps, if they went to this castle place, they might come to terms together.

"When does he want to go?" she asked.

"He was going this afternoon. He asked me to go with him but I didn't say definitely. Now I don't know what he's going to do."

"Why don't you ring him up and tell him you're free to go today if he wants to, after all?" Alison suggested.

"No, I can't do that. It would look—"

Clare broke off, meaning that it would look to Ewan Burnett as if she were changing her mind about that proposal of his to pose as his girl-friend in a fortnight's time. It should have come naturally, at the time he had suggested it, and not by suddenly ringing him up on a Saturday midday.

Alison, however, took it to mean that Clare was trying to hide her feelings for him. Clare had always been very sensitive about showing her feelings for people.

"Why don't you ring him up and tell him everyone will be out and, as you've nothing in particular to do, it might help him to get his notes taken as quickly as possible?" Alison urged.

"My dear sweet infant, life is so simple for you. You could manage it and make it sound natural. But I wouldn't be able to. No, let it ride till Monday."

Alison's cheeks were suddenly scarlet.

"No, life is not simple for me by any means and I shouldn't have attempted to advise you, considering the mess my own life is in."

"Oh, I'm *sorry*, Ally, really I am!" Clare said. "But you make me forget about your trouble because you're so cheerful and happy. Alison, are you sure you wouldn't be wise to telephone Keith and try to patch it up? You may be wrong about that other girl, you know."

"No. It's over—all over!" Alison replied fiercely as she went out of the room.

Clare left her to get a head start, and went to tidy for lunch. When she went down to the dining-room it was empty. She found Alison with the children, sitting round the biggest coffee table in the lounge, on hassocks, eating a meal which, to say the least of it, looked different from the pedestrian type of good plain food which Susan usually served up.

"Fish envelopes," Alison said, quietly, with a puckish grin, "and my own version of rabbit food."

"What's rabbit food?" Mellie wanted to know.

"All that pretty stuff," Alison told her, indicating the tiny lettuce hearts and other colourful bits she had included.

"Did you know, Clare," Jayne said, importantly, "that you can have bits of orange and apple with salad? We never have anything with lettuce and Alison grows nice stuff, not soggy leaves."

"What you've got to answer for in four weeks' time!" Clare murmured darkly, taking her place by her sister's side and accepting her plate of food.

"Well, they're eating it and not pushing it around the edges of the plate," Alison murmured, with an eye on the listening Mellie.

"What's that glamorous pudding, for heaven's sake!" Clare gasped, eyeing Susan's best tall-stemmed glasses.

"I shall replace them if they come to grief," Alison said, calmly. "Meantime, it's exciting window-dressing and it counts. You'll see how the stuff will vanish!"

Clare stared blankly at the swiftly cleared plates and bowls. "Golly!" she said, very much impressed, especially when she discovered that what looked like highly unsuitable adult food was really only the normal fruit purée out of Susan's baby tins in the kitchen, but whipped up with egg whites, and garnished with sponge fingers and glacé cherries. She didn't know whether to laugh or to be indignant on behalf of the two duped children who were eating themselves silly.

They were finishing the meal when the telephone rang. It was Ewan Burnett.

"Clare, I forgot to ask you last night whether you were doing anything this afternoon after all," he said, apologetically. "If you do happen to be at a loose end and would care to go to Bodcarne with me I'd appreciate it."

Clare glanced at Alison who was nodding vigorously, guessing who it was on the line.

"As it happens, Mr. Burnett, I can come," Clare said, and was rewarded by a beaming smile from her sister. "Alison is taking the children out and I hadn't planned anything for myself."

Alison calmly cleared the debris of the meal while Clare made arrangements to be picked up at the end of the road, and felt that she had at least been able to help sort out Clare's love-life, even if her own was still in a tangle.

Clare put the telephone down.

"Well, I seem to have had my mind made up for me!" she said. "What do you want to get rid of me for, this afternoon? Is it a secret?"

"I don't want to get rid of you," Alison said, indignantly. "I'm only going out with the children."

Clare wished that she hadn't been forced into this.

As she strode down the road half an hour later she wondered what it would be like to be spending such an afternoon with Ewan Burnett.

She had brought her shorthand note-book and a supply of pencils and a sharpener, and she had compromised over her week-end clothes; a free swinging pleated skirt of fine grey check and a grey cardigan and short-sleeved sweater, as something midway between her office clothes and frankly easy week-end wear. Her flat shoes removed inches from her height and to Ewan Burnett—who had arrived early and was parked round a corner watching for her—she looked much younger than usual, and curiously vulnerable.

He was so struck with the change in her appearance that he questioned what he was doing and almost called the whole thing off. The only reason he didn't do so was the fact that this plan of his would bring them far closer together than any formal advances he might make. He knew Clare perhaps better than she gave him credit for.

He greeted her with his usual pleasant coolness, which at once put her at her ease, and all the way to Bodcarne he talked about his notes, his reason for the journey to the castle, and what he intended to do with his researches of the day. In fact, it was just another working afternoon, spent in the car on the site of their work.

It was when they were having tea together in the one restaurant the village boasted that Ewan said, looking up at the frowning ruin on the hill, "Clare, would you feel like giving up your work in the surgery?"

"What did you say?" she gasped.

"Shock treatment, wasn't it?" he smiled. "I meant it. Now I've really got your attention. All the afternoon you've been divided—where has the other half of your mind been?"

"I'm sorry if I seemed inattentive," she apologised. "I didn't think I had."

"Well, you haven't answered my question. Would you feel like giving up your work in the surgery? To work full time for me?"

"Oh, no, I couldn't do that!" she burst out. Then, realising how blunt that must sound to him she said, quickly, "What I mean is, I'm quite happy doing two jobs. Anyway, what would the doctors do? The Shaws have been friends of my cousin's family for so long—I couldn't let them down."

"Don't worry about that," he told her coolly. "If it came to the point I daresay I could find them someone to take your place."

"But I wouldn't want that," she

protested. "Why do you suddenly want this change, Mr. Burnett?"

"I have a number of things for you to do that there never seems time to fit in as it is. I remember full well that the job was only intended for part time. It was at first. Now things have changed."

"How?"

"There isn't any point in telling you if you're not willing to give up your work for Dr. Shaw."

"Look," said Clare, carefully, "I like having two jobs—such different jobs—it makes life much more interesting. I don't mean that either of them would bore me. I just like it that way. Can't we leave it like that?"

"Are you sure that you don't mean that you like working personally for Dr. Shaw so much that you don't want to leave him?" he asked, whimsically.

Because of his tone and his deprecating smile she held back the surge of anger at his thrust. It was none of his business what she felt for Dr. Shaw, and she had the hardest task in the world not to say so outright.

Instead she said, pacifically, because she

didn't want to have to change either of her jobs, "Dr. Shaw might well say the same about you, if he asked me to give up working at Wycherley Holt and help him and his father full-time."

That counter-thrust amused him and he laughed.

"I see. Forgive me, Clare, I shouldn't have said that. But I do want you to keep in mind that if ever you want to get out of work in the surgery (and it must be a lot harder than your work with me!) you can come back to the subject. Don't forget, I can afford to employ you full time."

He merely meant that the Shaws might (if rumours were to be believed) consider dispensing with her secretarial services, and she might find herself out of a job whereas she wouldn't be in that position with him. But he saw at once that he had made a mistake in putting the thought into words.

Nothing he could do would undo that unfortunate impression on her mind. She had an unforgiving look in her eyes as she got up from the table.

It wouldn't be politic to remind her now about the proposition he had put to her about posing as his girl-friend in the evenings so he let it go, and cursed himself for being so outspoken about the Shaws. He believed in his heart that she was more keen on Raymond Shaw personally than she had admitted. He would be lucky if he could persuade her to fall in with his plans, let alone the other things he had in mind to suggest to her later.

So no more was said about either her jobs or her new evening work on the way home. Instead, Ewan Burnett coaxed her into giving her views on her notes taken today. Clare always eased out, he had noticed, when the conversation was kept within the tight circle of work.

She was still a little ruffled, however, when she reached home and found to her surprise that Alison and the children hadn't returned. It was long past Mellie's bedtime, though Jayne had an extra half hour.

While she was standing in the empty lounge, fighting down the unwelcome thought that something might have happened to them, a car drew up outside, and the children's shrill voices and laughter came to her through the open windows.

She stared unbelievingly. It was Raymond Shaw's car, and he was there himself, laughing and gay, helping Alison and the children out.

5

D R. SHAW didn't come in with them. He drove off almost at once. Clare went to the door and opened it for them. The children were ecstatic.

"Clare, guess who took us out today?"

"It was super, super!" Mellie shouted, dancing up and down.

"Dr. Shaw—we knew you couldn't guess! And he bought us ice cream and took us for rides—"

"And I was sick and he didn't mind a bit—"

"And old Ally said—"

"Yes, well, let's get in the house," Alison said firmly, taking charge. "Now first of all, what did you both promise me? To be good and quiet and calm down or else we don't all go out with Dr. Shaw tomorrow. Remember?"

The children promptly shut up completely and, if Jayne scowled going upstairs, she certainly calmed down.

Alison smiled at Clare, but there was reservation in her smile. "Did you have a good day, dear?" she said.

"It was a working afternoon," Clare told her. "I thought you said you were just taking the children out on your own?"

"Yes, I did—but Dr. Shaw saw us walking to the bus stop and—" She broke off as there was sudden pandemonium up in the bathroom. "I'll tell you about it as soon as I've got them into bed," she said and, dumping the bags on the hall floor, she ran upstairs, taking off her outdoor things as she went.

Clare was going up after her to lend a hand with the children but decided against it. The children were all right with her when they weren't tired but, at the end of the day, Mellie and Jayne might just play off the adults one against the other. Clare had seen those two in action before.

She went instead to the kitchen to make some coffee and sandwiches for her and Alison to have after the children were tucked down.

She was tired, too, she had to admit. Ewan Burnett, in an enthusiastic mood, could walk miles, and they had been on their feet for over two hours and a half before he thought of knocking off and walking down to the village in search of tea.

She thought about Ewan Burnett to keep her thoughts from Raymond Shaw. It was no use, she told herself furiously, minding about the doctor taking Alison and the children out. It had been no secret to her that he doted on children and it was no use thinking it odd that he had bothered little about Mellie and Jayne until Alison had arrived.

So she turned over in her mind about Ewan and his sudden suggestion that she should work up at Wycherley Holt all the time.

As she cut bread and butter she faced the thought of never again going to the surgery, and very rarely even seeing Raymond Shaw. She knew she couldn't risk that. It didn't matter even if he never saw her as anything but his secretary; it was enough to be working with him, helping him.

She despised herself. There were plenty of men in the world. Why take a header for someone so self-contained, so blandly indifferent to her presence?

You've no pride, Clare Drury, she told herself. Why don't you play up to Ewan Burnett? Something might come out of it!

There was still the answer to be found for when he again approached the subject of pretending to be his girl-friend. Frankly she disliked the idea so much that she was tempted to turn it down out of hand. It might have been different if she had liked Ewan more. As it was, she couldn't whip up any feeling at all for him, neither great liking nor great disliking. Even his remark about money this afternoon was beginning to fade because she had to admit that there was some truth in it. Dr. Shaw often jokingly said he was so hard-up that he ought to dispense with a secretary—even a part-time one—and do the clerical work himself. Other doctors in the district were doing that already or getting their wives to do the job.

She thought of what it would be like to be married to Raymond, doing the work from that angle, and hastily thrust it out of her mind. It was lunacy to get so upset, with Alison likely to come down at any minute! Besides, it was becoming clear, if she only let herself admit it, that it might well be Alison acting as the doctor's secretary pretty soon.

Alison called her. "Come and say good-night to them, will you, Clare?"

She went slowly upstairs, wishing she could turn the clock back a week, two weeks. Then Alison had been about to become engaged to Keith, Susan had been there with the children, Clare had been happily dreaming that one day—some day —Raymond Shaw would see her as a girl, and not just someone in a white coat with a pencil at the ready to jot down his appointments. She hadn't realised then how happy she had been.

She bent over Mellie's cot and cuddled her.

"I love you, Auntie Clare," Mellie said virtuously, even gratuitously flinging in an "Auntie" without being asked.

"What for?" she asked suspiciously.

"I love everyone 'cos I'm happy and 'cos we're going out with Uncle Raymond tomorrow."

"Who said you could call him Uncle

Raymond?" Clare asked, outraged, catching Alison's smile of amusement.

"He did. He says Ally can call him Raymond, too."

"He also said," Alison put in, clearing the whole thing up, "that as the two families had known each other so long, he didn't see why we shouldn't all be on christian name terms. After all, he calls you Clare."

Clare buried her face in the child's soft neck and blew softly on the skin to tickle; then kissed Mellie and said goodnight.

"Be good, or else!" she warned, as she went out to the accompaniment of the child's contented chuckles.

After they had tucked Jayne in they went down to the lounge and started their supper.

"Oh, this is good," Alison said, lying back in her armchair. "I'm tired out. That man's terrifically energetic, isn't he?"

"I wouldn't know," Clare said. "I'm only his secretary. How did you come to be out with him?"

"Oh, yes, I was telling you—he came up behind us in his car and said he was going on a visit and he'd give us a lift.

He seemed surprised you weren't with us, Clare, so I told him where you were. Did it matter?"

"Why should it?"

"Oh, I don't know—he seemed so surprised, I wondered whether there was anything in your arrangement with him that stopped you working for Mr. Burnett on Saturday afternoons, so I played safe and said you'd gone out with a man-friend. I hope that was all right!"

"I can't think it would matter one way or the other to the doctor," Clare said, drily, but she was annoyed. She had repeatedly said that she would be free on Saturday, if the doctor wanted her. Still, he didn't seem to require her services, so why worry—why worry?

"Clare, how did it go?" Alison asked, eyeing her anxiously. "Was it nice, or just work?"

"Just work," she said, briefly.

"Oh." Alison sounded so disappointed.

"Now just what did that mean?" Clare asked.

Alison spread her hands.

"Can't manage my own love-life but that's no reason why I shouldn't have a go at fixing yours, is it? You do like this Ewan Burnett, don't you?"

"Now what put that idea in your head?" Clare demanded.

"I don't know. Just got the feeling. What's he like? Describe him to me."

Clare did her best. "Tall, distinguished, elegant. Cultured way of speaking. Aloof, usually, and courted by half the mothers in the county (according to Susan) because he's wealthy and a bachelor."

"Sounds rather nice."

"Except that I couldn't imagine him kissing a girl, or having fun on holiday, or getting his mind off his work long enough to consider the problem of raising a family," Clare said, wryly.

"These things come," Alison comforted. "Clare, don't feel bound to come out with us tomorrow, if there's a date suggested— well, I mean, if Mr. Burnett had wanted you to go out with him tomorrow—"

"He didn't even mention it," Clare said, "but if you want to go out with Dr. Shaw, without me, it's okay. I'll have the kids, if you like."

Alison's astonishment was completely unfeigned.

"Don't be silly. It's only to take the children out that he suggested it, and he mentioned you being with us, today, so I do think it would look rather odd if you didn't come, unless you have some other date, that is."

"I should have been smart and said I had, shouldn't I?" Clare retorted.

"Don't you want to come out with us and Dr. Shaw, then?" Alison asked, plainly at a loss.

"Darling, I wouldn't really want to see my boss at the week-end, now would I? Don't you think I see enough of him during the week?"

But she likes going out with Ewan in off-times, Alison reasoned. That seemed to clinch it. Ewan Burnett was the one Clare was keen on, the one who never saw her as anything but a secretary. That was why the only time he had asked her out was a working half day. It seemed to clinch it so strongly that Alison had no doubts at all, and resolved to rope in Dr. Shaw to help Clare.

It was raining when they woke up next morning. A light rain that petered out by the time breakfast was over and, surprisingly, it turned out to be a hot day.

Alison, with her usual efficiency, had not only dusted and tidied the place while Clare had been making the beds, but she had got the picnic baskets ready. She had made sandwiches the night before and wrapped them in plastic bags and popped them in the fridge.

Raymond Shaw drove up at nine-thirty.

"He said ten," Alison remarked ruefully. "He's awfully eager for his picnic, isn't he?"

The children weren't quite ready so Alison invited him into the house, and showed him into the lounge.

"I'll find Clare," she said, and went to call her.

"I'm up here!" Clare sounded irritable. "Jayne's admitted to hiding one gumboot but won't say where it is! I'll be down in a jiff."

Alison chuckled and explained to Dr. Shaw.

"I'll go and get the picnic baskets," she said.

It struck her that Raymond Shaw didn't look quite so happy this morning. He was standing listening to Clare's voice trying alternately to cajole and bully Jayne into finding the gumboot.

Presently she clattered downstairs and burst into the lounge.

"The little brute was sitting on it!" she exclaimed, and then she saw that Alison wasn't in the room; just the doctor.

"Oh, hello," she said awkwardly, pulling up short. It was all very fine for Alison so easily to call him Raymond but, for Clare, it was an impossibility.

Besides, he looked so different today. In his open-necked short-sleeved green shirt and brown corduroy slacks, a tangerine husky sweater slung over his shoulder, he might have been a stranger standing there. His hair was ruffled in an unfamiliar way and she saw, beyond his shoulder, that his car, standing at the kerb, had the hood down, which explained his wind-blown appearance.

"Hello, Clare," he said, and he, too, didn't appear entirely at his ease. "Having trouble with Jayne?"

"Trouble? Oh, no, this is the usual nonsense when we're about to go out for the day. I'll find Alison."

"Just a minute, Clare. Where were you yesterday?"

"Why?" she asked him.

Alison, passing by the half open door, saw that neither of them looked really friendly. Puzzled, she stood there, hesitating. What was wrong with those two?

"Clare, I expected you to be with Alison and the children. I had no idea you wouldn't be with them."

"Did it matter?" she retorted.

"Well, yes, I think it did. I expected you to be in the party. Alison told me that you were out with your boy-friend, but I didn't even know you had one!"

"I don't know what Alison thinks she's doing. I don't understand any of it. If you want to go out with my sister Alison, why don't you? Surely you don't want me to go along and keep an eye on the children— or is that the whole idea?"

"Clare, please! I only wanted to know where you were," he said, still in that odd, awkward tone.

"I've no objection to your knowing. I was out with Ewan Burnett."

She hadn't meant to say it like that. She had meant to add that it was a working

97

afternoon but he didn't give her the chance.

"Burnett! Why didn't you say so in the first place?" he exploded.

"Because no one asked me," Clare reminded him, with heavy patience. "Now, don't you think we'd better make a start before the children get into any more mischief?"

Alison had them ready, sitting on the floor of the hall, each clutching a little bucket and spade.

"What are those for?" Clare gasped.

"We decided on Padcross, don't you remember, Clare?" Alison said, not looking at her sister, but busy on her task of lifting a picnic basket and getting the children to their feet. "It isn't the seaside but it's the next best thing. Part of the shore of the lake has some quite fine sand, and it keeps them amused."

Dr. Shaw moved forward quickly to help Alison with the basket and he lifted Mellie up on to his shoulder. Clare noticed the speed of his action. Never in their association had he raced forward to help her lift anything but, to be fair, she had always made it plain that she was the most capable, independent secretary he and his father had ever had or were ever likely to have.

She went out to the kitchen to see that all the gas and water taps were turned off and the windows all shut and the doors bolted. Then she let herself out of the front door.

Alison had meantime settled herself in the back of the car with the children, leaving the front seat empty beside the doctor.

"Why aren't you sitting here?" Clare asked. If, she reasoned to herself, Alison was beginning to like the doctor, there was no point in staying at the back with the children.

"If anyone's going to keep these scamps in order," Alison laughed, "it had better be me."

"Do you mind, Dr. Shaw?" Clare asked, at a loss. They all seemed so friendly together, and she was queerly shy, now that he was in their home party.

"Call him Raymond," the children shouted.

The doctor looked impatient now.

"For heaven's sake, do, Clare," he said

and started the car up almost before she had got in. "It will make it easier all round."

Charming, she told herself. It was like being at work again, with a full surgery, the telephone jangling all the time and the doctor becoming more impatient with her every minute.

It was Alison, after all, who talked to him, crosswise from behind Clare. Alison who kept the children quiet by giving five marks for every time they spotted a grey car and ten for each time they saw a red one. Alison it was who kept up the happy note so that it was difficult to resist the fun from the back seat.

Padcross was a town built on a hill. As they halted at the traffic lights of the tortuous cross-roads at the top, they could look out over the roofs of the town to where a lake shimmered in the sunshine and the sand was like a yellow crescent round its rim. Already there were one or two sails on it.

"I can see the sea," Jayne shouted, standing up.

Clare's heart turned over but Alison saved the situation. She held on to Jayne's dress and gently tugged her back into her seat.

"Gently, sweetie. We don't want anything horrid to happen now we've arrived, do we? Let's sit quiet and good while we go down the hill."

Yet a sense of premonition stayed with Clare. Those children were all right so long as Alison's eye was on them. But what a responsibility! No wonder Susan had been so glad to get away for a bit of peace and quiet!

She thought resolutely of Susan and Tony and wondered where they would be. In Italy, of course, and at this time of the year the beaches wouldn't be packed. Hot sunshine and warm blue sea and quiet . . .

Dr. Shaw swooped down to the bottom of the hill and through narrow back streets to the cobbled lane that led down to the car park.

"Oh, could we take the car down to the shore?" Alison begged. "Some cars do park fairly near the water and it would be a help. We wouldn't have to carry all the things then."

"Can we paddle?" Mellie cried.

"Can we swim?" Jayne wanted to know.

"Yes, I expect so," the doctor said, his good humour apparently restored. "Do anything you like so long as you don't get into mischief."

He played ball with them for a while near the parked car. Then Alison said they could build in the sand before lunch. She started a castle for them while Clare got the baskets out of the car. But while she was spreading the cloth there was a sudden sharp shower of rain.

Clare and Alison helped the doctor to put the hood up but the rain persisted and finally they were driven to eat their lunch in the car. It was a messy business with the two children but Alison kept the party bright and, after lunch, the doctor drew pin-men pictures and kept the children laughing until the rain stopped.

Watery sunshine drew people out from the shelter of their cars but it was warm, so Alison decided to let the children paddle before an early tea.

While she was getting the children ready to paddle the doctor said suddenly to Clare: "Come to the top and see the view over the valley while the youngsters are in the water. It's too steep to take them and I expect Alison will be glad of a rest."

Clare looked at Alison who had glanced quickly up at them from where she knelt by Mellie's side.

"Oh, I don't think so," Clare said. "I'll stay with the children and give my sister a break. Take her with you. She doesn't know the district and I do."

He looked frustrated.

"Clare, if you must have it bluntly, there's something I want to discuss with you, personal and private. I know Alison won't mind if we walk while we talk."

"No, of course not," Alison said quickly, but Clare could sense her sharp surprise.

Raymond Shaw took Clare's arm and walked her briskly up off the beach to the path through the woods. It sloped in zigzag fashion, a narrow path washed smooth by the rains. Usually the bare clay was hardened by swift drainage but today it was treacherous. The recent rain had left it slippery and the exposed roots of trees were a trap to the unwary. Once she caught her foot in a protruding root and he took her arm to save her from pitching forward, forgetting to let go again when she had steadied herself. She tried to pull away but he apparently didn't notice.

"Clare, I want to talk about Burnett," he said, abruptly, displeasure in his voice. "Why do you have to go on working for the fellow? Do you need full employment to that extent?"

"What *do* you mean?" she cried, turning to face him.

"Look out, it's dangerous on this path!" he warned her sharply, as she nearly lost her footing again. "You must know very well what I mean, Clare! I thought you were living with your cousin Susan and just needed morning work to keep you busy and interested. If you need a full time job why didn't you say so?"

"Why?"

"Because you could have come to us in the afternoons to type my father's manuscript, instead of our having to rely on an agency for it."

"I never thought about it," she said, frankly. "I know your father has published several books but, every time I offer to help him in surgery, you always say he likes to work alone, so I took it that his independence included his writing as well."

"Well, what about it Clare? Why don't you come to us full time and leave this Burnett chap?"

"But I like working for Ewan Burnett! Why should I leave him?"

"Because he—oh, well, never mind," Raymond Shaw began in a tone which had a tinge of contempt in it. "If you've made up your mind to continue working for him, nothing *I* say will make any difference."

They had reached the top now and she felt safe enough underfoot to break away from him and face him squarely again.

"I don't understand what all this is about," she said, at last. "Of course I'll listen to you, on any reasonable subject. You know that! But why suddenly take against my other employer when you've always said you didn't mind who else I worked for?"

"That was before I found out things about him. Even then I didn't think it was worth mentioning. To be frank, I thought you'd get tired of two jobs—it can't be easy—and I hoped you'd give up working for Burnett. But now it's different," he went on, more quietly, and very earnestly. "Clare, you do see that it's your welfare I'm thinking about, don't you?"

"My welfare! What's that got to do with it? Are you sure it isn't because of something my sister Alison has said? She told me she'd been talking about him to you."

"Alison wouldn't say anything that wasn't true, I'm sure," he said, swiftly.

"Well, in that case, why don't you just think about my sister Alison's welfare and leave me to take care of myself? So long as I work adequately for you in the mornings surely I can be left to decide what I want to do in the afternoons?"

He looked at her in a baffled sort of way.

"You think I'm interfering, Clare?"

"I couldn't be blamed if I did, could I? What have you got against Mr. Burnett, I should like to know?"

"Would you, would you really? Are you sure you would listen? I always thought you were such a reasonable young woman. I never thought that I'd hear that you were going out with the fellow!"

"So that's what's bothering you!" she

exploded. "Really! What is more to the point is that he wants me to leave your employ and work for him full-time."

"Does he! Clare, you're not going to do any such thing, are you?"

"Not while you want me to stay on. You ought to know me better than that!" she said, indignantly. "But you have said, at times, that you really couldn't afford to keep a secretary, and if you ever find that you have to dispense with my services—"

"Oh, what a lot of rot, Clare! That's only my father's idea of a bit of fun, a joke! Or did you hear it from Burnett? Of course we're not that hard-up. My father makes a good deal of money out of his medical text-books and, if you must know, I happen to have a private income, and in case Burnett casts doubts on where it came from, I got it honestly, inherited from my mother."

"Really, Dr. Shaw!" she said, her cheeks scarlet.

She was unhappy at the way the conversation had drifted. She had no desire to be at loggerheads with Dr. Shaw and she found herself wishing that he hadn't guessed what Ewan Burnett had said (or, rather, hinted) about the finances of the two doctors. She also wished that Raymond Shaw hadn't spoken in such a way. It wasn't like him to lose his temper so easily.

"I'm sorry, Clare," he said, swiftly. "I shouldn't have blown up like that. But to think of that bounder Burnett saying things—"

"I didn't say he did!" she found herself forced to protest.

"No, you didn't have to. I can read it in your face. Besides, we've heard rumours of it from other sources. And to think I was squeamish about giving you reasons for my warning you against him."

"All right, don't have any scruples about telling me just what you know about him. Don't you think you owe it to me, after having hinted so much?"

"It's just whispers about him, from people we know and can trust. But you must see that no one locally has accepted him, or even likes him, and there's no smoke without fire."

"Rumours!" She almost sniffed. "Local rumours! That's because he's rich and got a lot of time to spare and people don't understand how writers can make a lot of money sometimes. I like him," she said, perversely.

She hated herself for saying it, because it wasn't really true. But something in Raymond Shaw's manner made her want to hit out at him and defend Ewan Burnett. After all, Ewan Burnett had been kindness itself to her and Raymond Shaw was just being interfering.

"Do you really mean that, Clare?" he asked, sharply.

He tilted her face up to him to look more closely at her. That little action tipped the scales. She at once resented the turbulent way her pulses raced at the mere touch of his finger under her chin. Unreasonably she hated him for being able to upset her so, when all the time he didn't care one bit about her, and was, in fact, interested only in Alison.

"Yes, I do, and you know I don't say things I don't mean! You must know by now that I'm independent—"

"Oh, I know that all right!" he replied, removing his finger from her chin and thrusting his hands into his pockets.

"—and I like to make up my own mind about what I do and with whom I do it."

"I can see that I would have done better not to say a word," he said, but without any rancour in his tone. "We'd better be getting back or the others will wonder where we are. Take a look at the view before we go down, so that Alison won't suspect we've been having a row."

Alison, Alison, always it was what Alison would think and say, Clare thought hotly. Then she despised herself for thinking those things about her sister. If Alison wanted Raymond Shaw she could have him, and welcome to him! There was always Ewan Burnett, she told herself furiously.

They made the difficult journey down to the lake again in an unfriendly silence. Occasionally Clare's shoes skidded and he automatically looked back and put out a hand, but she knew he had withdrawn any friendliness he had shown her.

Sick misery stuck like a lump in her throat. Why did she have to be in love with a man she could only quarrel with like this. A man who was so full of her sister that the one reason he wanted Clare herself alone was to censure her movements.

Clare asked herself if she could have managed this meeting up here in a different way, whether she could have been easier with him. The answer shocked her. Yes, she could have, if she hadn't been in love with him. Her feelings for him made an artificial barrier, so that she could no longer be natural with him. The knowledge of his interest in Alison made things difficult, too.

The only thing to do was to get out, as Ewan Burnett had suggested. How could she even enjoy working with the doctor now, if things were going to be like this?

Perhaps his thoughts were on the same lines, for he turned suddenly and looking up at her with appeal in his eyes, he said persuasively, "Clare, don't let's be like this. Do we have to be?"

She wondered afterwards what would have happened between them if there hadn't been a sudden commotion down by the lakeside.

They both heard it simultaneously and turned to look over a ridge of bushes which gave them a clear view of the place where the car was parked, and where Alison had been with the children.

A crowd of people had collected and some were wading out into the water.

An awful fear clutched at Clare as she remembered her earlier premonitions.

"It's one of the children, I think!" she gasped.

"I can't see clearly what's happening but we'd better get down quickly and see," Raymond said urgently.

She followed him, slithering and slipping. He reached the firm ground at the foot of the path long before she did and, when she arrived at the bottom with a little rush of loose stones, he was running across the strip of sand.

He was carrying Mellie in his arms, people milling all around him, when Clare reached the car.

"Give her air!" he was shouting. "Stand back—it's all right. I'm a doctor!"

Alison was there, and someone else was hanging on to Jayne. Clare took over the care of Jayne and explained who she was. She was almost shut off by the small crowd from Raymond and Alison but she could just see Alison leaning into the car and getting out Raymond's bag. The next moment she saw Alison wrapping the car rug round Mellie, being busy in the way she had been trained to be. Her head and Raymond's were close together, shutting out everyone, even Clare herself.

"How did it happen, Jayne?" Clare asked the child. "Where were you?"

Jayne looked mutinous and wouldn't answer.

"Jayne," Clare said, leading the child off to a little mound of short grass and sitting her down on it, squatting down herself in front of the child and holding her hands. "It's important, honey. What happened? Tell Clare."

"I ran away," Jayne said at last.

"What for?"

"Don't know," Jayne said simply.

"Where was Alison?" Clare pursued, trying to get some sort of picture.

"Looking for Mellie," Jayne replied unwillingly.

The people were beginning to melt away now; everything seemed to be under control and there was no further excitement.

Clare heard someone say, "Fancy those

other two leaving that young girl with two such tiresome children—they ought to be ashamed of themselves!" And, as she passed, the speaker, an elderly woman with a severe face, glared at Clare.

"Were you both being naughty?" Clare persisted.

Jayne seemed surprised. "Yes!" she admitted.

"Oh, Jayne! Now look what you've done."

Jayne was indignant. "Wasn't me," she said furiously.

"You mean it was Mellie's fault?"

"Horrid Clare, you don't understand."

"Then tell me!"

"I want my Mummy!" Jayne began to bawl.

"Now do stop that, darling. Listen, what made you run away if Mellie was already lost? Were you trying to find her?"

"No, we wanted Raymond, but he'd gone away with you. So we said we'd hide and Alison would have to go and call him to find us. Only she didn't. She got cross because we ran away. Why did Ally get cross?"

Why, indeed? Cross because Raymond

Shaw had deliberately taken Clare away to talk to her alone and privately?

That was the only reason Clare could think of. She blamed herself for not being more firm and sticking to her first refusal to go off for that walk with him.

He had now settled Mellie in the back of the car and was coming over towards her.

She got up and took Jayne's hand.

"Come on, we'll find a nice cup of milk for you," she said comfortingly.

"I think," the doctor said, as he came up to them, "that we'll be getting home. Mellie's suffering from shock. It's bed for her. Pity the day turned out like this," he added, picking up Jayne and carrying her to the car.

But he didn't look very much put out, to be packing up that disastrous picnic and taking them all back home, Clare thought as she followed him.

Alison was already sitting in the back, with Mellie. They had wrapped the child up in rugs and spread her along the back seat. She certainly looked very white and sick.

"How is she?" Clare asked.

"She'll be all right," Alison said briefly, and she didn't even look up at her sister.

Now what was wrong, Clare asked herself, frustrated. There was a distinct atmosphere in the car. Had Raymond Shaw been sharp with Alison for allowing this to happen? There was no handling him these days, he was so prickly.

"What happened, Alison?" Clare pursued. "I couldn't get much out of Jayne."

"I didn't see what happened," Alison said quietly. "I've already explained to Raymond—I lost Mellie and was looking for her when Jayne broke away. I went after Jayne and, while I was chasing her, some people said a child had fallen in the water. It was Mellie. Then Raymond came running and took her from someone."

It was all very odd. Alison usually marshalled the children so that this sort of thing just couldn't happen. She sat in the front beside Raymond, with Jayne on her lap. Jayne was now so subdued that there seemed little chance of anything else happening that day.

He drove grimly home. It wasn't such an easy run back. They had to crawl up

116

the hill into Padcross in a long line of other cars returning, because of the deterioration of the day and, before they had crawled through Padcross town, the rain was coming down again, more heavily this time.

Jayne started to cry. She hated the rain drumming on the roof of the car.

"Hush, darling, you'll wake Mellie!" Clare murmured.

"Want to wake Mellie! Mellie! Wake up!" Jayne shrieked.

"Cut it out, Jayne!" the doctor said shortly.

Jayne was so surprised that she did stop crying and sat glaring at him for some time.

Finally, she said, leaning forward, "I don't like you. Not going to call you Raymond any more."

He grinned briefly at her.

"Please yourself, old dear, but don't wake Mellie up. If you do, she'll be so cross, she won't let you go to sleep when you go to bed, and you know how you hate that."

Jayne ignored that threat completely.

"I don't like you. Neither does our Alison."

"Jayne, how could you!" Alison said very irately from the back seat. "Raymond, she's tired and cross. Perhaps you'd better stop and let me have her over in the back with me."

Clare quite unreasonably resented that suggestion. It implied that she wasn't capable of handling the child.

"She'll be all right with me, Alison," she said. "You've got enough on your hands with Mellie."

The doctor glanced at her, signalled to cars behind him and pulled into the side.

"Put her over in the back, Clare. Here, I'll give you a hand," he said.

Jayne gave her an aggravating grin as she was transferred from the front of the car to the back seat.

As the doctor re-started the car Clare privately decided that she wouldn't come out on one of these outings again. She had never felt more in the way in her life before. Those two had so much in common, not the least of which was that they both had the knack of handling Jayne and Mellie, while she herself hadn't.

She hardly caught the doctor's words as he said, bending down over the gears to pick up a map that had dropped to the floor, "Besides, I want to talk to you!"

"If it's the same subject as before," Clare began frigidly, "then there's no more to be said. In any case, this is hardly the time or the place."

"What does that mean, Clare?" He asked, as he worked his way back into the mainstream of the traffic.

It was very quiet in the back of the car now. She glanced behind. Jayne's eyelids were drooping sleepily and she cuddled her face into Alison's shoulder. Alison was doing her best to appear to be thinking of other things and not listening to their conversation.

"You know what I mean," Clare said. "Why don't you leave it alone? It doesn't matter, anyway."

"It does, you know," he said. "For heavens' sake, Clare, there's never time or opportunity in the surgery and I'm always called out before I can have a word with you after the door's closed on the last patient. Then you clear off to Burnett's place in the afternoon. When else *can* I talk to you?"

"You've talked to me, up the hill. And it seems to me that if you really want a change made then I think that Ewan Burnett's idea is the better one."

"You can't mean that, Clare!" Raymond Shaw exploded. "Look here, I'll leave Alison to put the kids to bed. I'll drive you out somewhere and discuss this thing further. We've got to come to some sort of agreement."

"It isn't necessary and, anyway, I've had enough of today," Clare told him. "It's been a beastly day. Oh, it wasn't your fault. The weather didn't help and everything went wrong and I always think that when things are like that one should pack it up and not try to fight them. I meant what I said, you know, anyway."

Alison leaned forward. "Clare, I should do as he asks you. Go for a drive round. You can't discuss anything important like this with us all here."

"This isn't your problem, Alison. You don't even know what it's all about!" Clare told her sister firmly.

Alison subsided, a hurt look on her face.

She said no more. Raymond folded his lips in a straight line, as he did when a patient argued with him or wouldn't take advice. He liked his own way and so did she. It was as well that they weren't going to be other than employer and employee—they would always be clashing, she told herself.

But it didn't make her feel any better. Excitement shot through her as she thought, for a fleeting moment, of what it would be like if Alison weren't there—just the doctor and herself, and they had quarrelled and were making it up after the quarrel.

The heat of her emotions decided her. When they reached the house she decided that if there was nothing she could do to help she wouldn't even stay there.

Alison took Mellie up to bed. The doctor got his bag and left Clare to bring in the debris of their picnic. She could hear him talking to Alison upstairs; Mellie briefly crying, but only cross crying; Mellie hated being disturbed when she had once been to sleep.

With one of Susan's big aprons on, Clare began to repair the kitchen fire, and to start an evening meal. She took a savage pleasure in washing-up, setting the table, anything to keep busy and not think of those two upstairs. After all, if something had happened between them today it might well be because of her own presence, and now they had a good opportunity of setting things to rights.

She had just poured an omelette mixture into the big buttered pan over the flame, when the telephone rang.

Raymond was coming downstairs with Alison. They were talking about Mellie.

"After that shot, she should sleep and be all right in the morning," he was saying. "Don't worry, Alison, it wasn't your fault, I'm sure. Don't think I don't realise what a responsibility they are, those two kids!"

As Clare lifted the receiver she saw Alison's swift warm smile for Raymond and, in the mirror she caught a side view of his face. More pleasure was in it than had been there the whole day.

It was the last straw that tipped the scale. Ewan Burnett was on the end of the line.

"Oh, is that you, Clare? At last! Where

have you been? I've been phoning you on and off all day!"

"What for? Did you want me urgently?" she asked, wondering what could have happened to cause him to telephone on a Sunday anyway.

There was a little silence and she thought she heard him say, "I always—" He broke off, and began again, more firmly, as if he were carefully selecting his words. "I'm sorry to bother you on a Sunday, but it occurred to me that you might be at a loose end and so was I, and that you might care to reconsider that dinner date with me that never materialised. What about tonight, Clare?"

At any other time she would have thought of a good excuse for a swift refusal, but tonight her whole world had tipped upside down.

In the distance she heard Alison say, "Well, we've plenty of eggs in the house. Look, Clare's started an omelette. Why don't you stay and have a bite with us?"

That finally decided her. She would not, whatever else happened, be a third party again tonight. If they wanted a meal together they were welcome!

"I'd love to come out to dinner with you," she told Ewan Burnett, with what appeared to be real pleasure in her voice.

6

"I THOUGHT we'd go to Illingfold, for a change," Ewan said mildly, as he settled her in his big car at the end of the road and drove smoothly away. "You look very nice, Clare. I'm so glad you could come!"

He was so nice and agreeable and formal and peaceful—yes, that was the word: peaceful. Clare thought of all the undercurrents of earlier in the day; Alison and the way she avoided Clare's eyes, and the doctor and his passionate outburst about something which, Clare told herself, was really no business at all of his. And by comparison she welcomed Ewan's manner and everything about him.

She smiled at him, and said, "It was a nice surprise. I thought you were visiting writing friends this evening."

"Actually I was," he admitted, "but earlier today I heard that the Hewitts would be there."

The Hewitts. She wracked her brains,

trying to remember who the Hewitts were. Someone she ought to know, that was clear.

"You must remember, Clare! The mother and daughter who are threatening my future peace of mind," he said, frowning a little. He didn't like to have to explain to her what he meant. She was supposed to be so interested in him as a person that it shouldn't have been necessary for him to have to prompt her.

"Oh, yes," she said. Those people! So that was what he wanted her to go to dinner with him tonight for—to discuss that particular scheme of his.

"What are they like?" she asked, to give herself time. What should she say to him? He had said she had two weeks' grace in which to consider the matter, but now those wretched people were making an earlier move so he would want an answer.

"Oh, Mrs. Hewitt is a charming person, in the ordinary way," he said, driving smoothly through the now almost deserted Padcross, and down the hill, past the ill-fated lake. "Francine is a pretty little thing, quite charming, but rather a worrying type to consider as one's future

126

wife," and he almost but not quite shuddered.

"I see," she said. "I should have thought you'd be better off with someone like her, though. With a mother like that, you'd have a good combination for all your entertaining. They know all your writing friends, don't they?"

"Oh, yes, I agree from that point of view Francine would be a very good choice, if I hadn't thought of what sort of wife I would like, and she doesn't happen to fit my idea of a suitable companion."

She was silent. He was in that odd mood again, the one he had been in, the day he had first suggested this.

She knew she ought to keep her mind on this thing, but they were going round the lake, and her thoughts would keep going back to earlier in the day, and the way Raymond Shaw had looked back at her, just before they had realised there was a commotion on the shore.

What could he have been going to say, she asked herself feverishly. She wished she could turn back the clock, just to find out. Why should he be so keen to be friends with her, if it was Alison he cared about? Wisely keeping in with someone who would be his sister-in-law?

She hadn't thought of that before, and she was shocked at the wave of horror that swept over her. She didn't want to be Raymond Shaw's sister-in-law. That would be too much torture. If she couldn't be closer to him under her own steam, she didn't want to have to see or hear of him again; certainly not be in the family yet on the outside, watching him being in love with Alison every day, perhaps starting a family of their own.

"What's the matter, Clare?" Ewan asked, rather testily. "What are you looking at the lake for like that?"

"Like what?" she gasped. How much had she given away in her face, while she had been thinking of Raymond Shaw?

"As if you expected to see a monster crawl out of it. You haven't asked me yet, what sort of a wife I had pictured for myself."

She resisted the temptation to answer that one, by reminding him he had always insisted he was the bachelor type. "You rather pride yourself on being a bachelor, don't you?" she smiled.

"A man can change, especially when one woman shows him how nice life could be, if he could consider himself in the light of a husband."

He looked so put out at having to say that in so many words that she was sorry for him. She hadn't realised until now that a lot of his trouble was shyness. While he was engaged on his work he had all the confidence in the world, but just leave him alone with a pretty girl and he looked ready to bolt.

"I shouldn't worry about it, Mr. Burnett."

"Ewan," he corrected her. "Is it so hard to say?"

"Ewan," she repeated. "I think you worry too much about these things. Can't you be nice and friendly with this Francine, yet make it clear that you're not contemplating marriage?"

He glanced at her, as he pulled up at the crossroads and waited for a single-decker bus to go through. His glance was filled with frustration.

"You don't understand at all, do you, Clare?" he exploded, and as the crossroads were clear, he gave his attention to driving again. "You haven't said what bothered you about the lake, either. You weren't just idly looking at it, were you?"

"Oh, Ewan!" she sighed. "Well, we were here this morning and one of my cousin's children fell in. You can hardly expect me not to look at the wretched place as we passed it, can you?"

"Good gracious! So that's where you were! Oh, dear, how trying! Are the children always doing things like that?"

"More or less," she agreed cheerfully. "Anyway, no harm was done. She's tucked up in bed now. My sister's looking after her. She's wonderful with children."

"Oh, that's a comfort. I had the awful thought that you were going to say you couldn't come to me because you had to look after those children."

"No, no, it really isn't my line, actually."

"Don't you like children, Clare?"

It was such an odd question, coming from him, that for the moment she couldn't think of a reply. "Of course I like children," she said at last. "But they play me up at times. They never (or almost never) do that with my sister."

"What made you go out with them today then?"

"Well, I could hardly refuse to go with her and help her with them, could I, as I had nothing better to do?" she said shortly, wishing she hadn't mentioned the lake or even looked at it.

"You think I'm questioning you a lot, don't you, but you see, Clare, I want to know everything about you. I have to, don't I, if you consent to do what I asked you to, and step in as my—er—possible future fiancée." He allowed a little pause, then he took the plunge, and said rapidly, "And I would like to know now, my dear, if you feel you can do it. Before we reach Illingfold, that is."

"Why?"

"I'll tell you why, when you say yes or no."

She hated feeling driven to make up her mind, but quite suddenly the idea offered an escape from all her other problems. If she said yes, she would have a very good reason for going off like this with Ewan Burnett, without the distressing scene she had left behind at the house. Raymond Shaw looking quietly angry to find that she

131

had just that minute agreed to go out with Ewan Burnett of all people when she must have heard Alison invite Raymond to share their supper with them. Alison quietly angry because Clare had accepted the invitation, because she knew the doctor wouldn't stay there alone with her to supper.

As if it were someone else answering for her, Clare heard herself say, "Yes, I've thought it over, and I'll agree to your suggestion, if it will really help you, Ewan."

He seemed so relieved that she wondered.

"Now, why did you want to know in such a hurry?" she asked him. "You remember you did give me two weeks in which to think it over."

"Yes, my dear, I know that, and at the time I thought I had that much leeway in which to turn round. But you know, Mrs. Hewitt is a very determined woman, and she knows enough about me to realise that if I said I was otherwise engaged, it wouldn't be true. So I have to have, well, proof—in the person of yourself. Now—this evening, I'm afraid. I do hope this isn't as distasteful to you as your expression suggests. It could be quite a pleasant way of spending Sunday evening, you know!"

"Why didn't you tell me before, that we were going to run into those people tonight?" she fumed. "I'd have put on something else."

He looked at the quiet little navy two-piece she was wearing, and smiled slightly. "That is my idea of how you should look tonight, Clare. Quietly elegant. You'll realise why, when you see Mrs. Hewitt and Francine."

Illingfold was a prosperous market town, with one large hotel where civic functions were held—The Three Drovers. It had started life as a coaching inn, and still preserved the old frontage, looking out over the market square, but the owners had acquired a large piece of land at the back for their modern extensions, and they had thoughtfully included a very large car-park.

Ewan drove through the old archway where coaches had once squeezed through, and parked in a quiet corner. She waited while he fussed about whether other cars

133

could scratch his paintwork. Unlike Raymond Shaw's, Ewan Burnett's car was worth fussing about.

He laid a hand on her arm as she was about to get out. "Just a moment, Clare— I've got something to show you."

He drew out a velvet case and opened it, to reveal a string of pearls.

Clare had no means of knowing their value. She had never possessed any really good jewellery. But she knew Ewan Burnett and his expensive tastes, and instinct told her that this was worth a great deal.

"Very nice," she said, because it appeared to be expected of her.

He smiled slightly. That casual comment appealed more to him than Francine's squeal of excitement and delight would have done.

"It's for you, Clare. May I put it on?"

"For me! Now wait a minute—" she began.

"Oh, I expected a fuss about accepting a gift from me. I know your independent spirit. But just the same, I wish you'd accept it from me."

"If you want to lend it to me, to embellish my appearance for the part you're asking me to play, that will be different, and I could understand that!" she said spiritedly.

"Ye-es," he sighed, half to himself. "I knew this would be difficult. I'm afraid that won't work, Clare. In the first place, I never lend anything. You'll find that out in time. I must possess or give—or not at all. That's me. No half measures. It can't be a birthday gift—my files tell me your birthday isn't within shooting range. Then we'll have to say it's a gift of appreciation for what you are about to undertake for me."

"But it's just part of my job, and I don't want any payment for it," she protested.

"It may be a far more exacting job than you had bargained for, and it would give me pleasure to think I had in part compensated for your efforts. Do give me that pleasure, Clare," he really pleaded this time.

She half shrugged. "All right, but supposing I don't feel I can continue with what is, after all, a deception? If you agree that I may give these back in that case, then I'll accept them."

He pulled a face, but agreed, and put them on her. Their touch was slightly and disconcertingly warm to her bare neck, and they made her feel that everything else about her appearance was wrong.

Irritated, she got out of the car before he could say anything else, and she missed his fleeting look of disappointment.

He locked the car and followed her into the hotel. The restaurant looked curiously bare. It was early, but as Ewan told her, sensing her surprise, it would fill very quickly.

He secured for them a quiet corner table and carefully chose the wine. People began coming in very quickly now.

Clare slipped off the little jacket. The dress beneath it was sleeveless, cut very high at the throat in front, which made a perfect dark foil for the pearl necklace. The back of the dress was cut away, and cool; just right for the sort of evening when she wasn't sure what entertainment could be expected.

Ewan eyed her approvingly. "You really are very lovely, Clare," he said.

"Is that part of the act, Ewan? Have we started already, without rehearsal?"

She only meant it for her own clarification, but he looked curiously hurt. She was puzzled.

"What is it? I only wanted to know."

"I suppose I should say we have started, Clare," he said, "as I see our friends approaching now."

She didn't look round, but quietly patted her hair in the great mirror beside her, and caught sight of a party approaching. An extremely well-groomed, well-preserved woman in her late fifties led the way; a woman with immaculately dressed silver hair, and an unnaturally unlined face. The woman was laughing a great deal with her companions, and her diamonds glittered with every movement. She wore a couturier dress of grey velvet, and a mink stole trailed casually over one arm.

Behind her was a pretty little blonde in a short blue dance dress. They would have to pass this table to get to their own, it was clear, and they had already spotted Ewan and were bearing down on him.

Ewan hastily got to his feet and greeted the older woman.

"Ewan darling!" she said effusively and

kissed him, and began introductions to the rest of her party, without having apparently noticed Clare.

Francine stood staring at Clare, and when he had a chance, Ewan introduced her. Clare fleetingly wondered how he would present her to these people, but Ewan was smooth, purposeful. He had a definite outlined plan which, for the moment, pushed his shyness into the background. Besides, Clare was his barrier against this scintillating, forceful woman and her pretty daughter.

"Miss Clare Drury, Mrs. Lattimore Hewitt," he said, yet somehow by his inflexion on Clare's name, he made it sound as if Clare were very special indeed to him.

Mrs. Hewitt apparently thought so, too. But her momentary hesitation fled before her brilliant smile and she made it plain that she considered that a bit of nonsense and that Ewan would surely ask her party to join him at his table.

Ewan, however, didn't, so she had to say that they had a table booked elsewhere, and they all sailed off to settle themselves round it. The other girl and the two men had apparently noticed nothing wrong, and the party chattered and laughed, and Mrs. Hewitt didn't once allow her glance to stray across to where Ewan was putting a hand over the table-cloth to touch Clare's.

"She didn't like me," Clare said. "Shouldn't you have asked them to join us?"

"That was hardly the idea," he said dryly. "We want to be alone, don't we?"

"Francine looked a very nice girl," Clare said, bothered somehow about all this. She should have had a chance of seeing these people first, before she undertook blindly such a curious job.

"Oh, she *is* a very nice girl!" he agreed cheerfully, as the wine came.

Clare waited while Ewan and the waiter went through the performance of tasting and approving, then the wine was poured and they were again alone, and Ewan raised his glass. "I think I may be permitted to toast the most beautiful girl I've ever seen!"

"Well, if you will sit with your back to everyone else," Clare said lightly.

"It wouldn't make any difference if I

could see everyone else in the room," he said gravely.

"Ewan, you must have rehearsed your part, and you never gave me a chance to rehearse mine," she protested.

"I'd rather you didn't say things like that, if we want this to succeed," he told her. "Besides, there are other things I want to say. First, I love you."

"You don't have to carry it too far!" she protested.

"Don't look like that, or Mrs. Lattimore Hewitt will think I'm suggesting something improper to you," he smiled. "She's watching, and wondering where I met you and how soon she can pump you for details about your past life. I hope you've got your background details ready."

"I haven't thought a thing about it, and I do wish you'd briefed me before this!"

"I could have done, if you'd said yes when I first suggested it. Even a day would have helped."

"It won't work, you know, Ewan. Besides, that Francine is really very pretty, and used to all this. I'm not. I live a very cosy, domestic sort of life. No thrills or excitements. I don't go out to dances much, and I don't ride or hunt or know any of the people that you know and they know."

"Now you're being snobbish, Clare."

"No. Practical, surely? At least you might have picked someone who could really play the part."

"I picked you, with my eyes wide open," he assured her. "Shouldn't you say something in answer to my remark about the way I feel about you? Don't ask me to repeat it. I couldn't. I had to work up to it as it was."

She frowned, because that had the ring of authenticity about it. But he was only playing a part, and it was his own suggestion, after all!

"What sort of actor would *you* make, not being able to repeat the performance?" she laughed. "What a shame, and you did it so nicely!"

"Well, Clare?"

"I'm no actress, honestly, Ewan. I don't know what to say! I'd know what to say if it were the real thing."

"Can't you pretend it is? It really means a great deal to me, and after all, it is only a bit of acting. Lots of people do it for a living! Go on, try! I've done my bit!"

The only way she could think of, to make it at all convincing, was to think of Raymond Shaw sitting there in Ewan's place, but for the life of her, she couldn't really see the doctor here, in this place, or in those evening clothes, with that air of distinction about him. She could imagine Raymond having a moonlight picnic in a boat, or having rough red wine in a cellar with candles stuck in bottle tops, and someone playing an accordion and—she could see him very clearly sitting hunched in the bucket seat of a car, feeding small children like hungry sparrows while he munched his own sandwiches.

The memory of this morning, that ought to have been so nice and somehow wasn't, brought tears to her brown eyes, and she lowered them.

"When people are really in love, they don't usually make pretty speeches," she said chokily. "They say all the wrong things, and they quarrel, and they don't mean it, and it hurts and hurts. Being really in love isn't really a suave, well-bred affair—not to people like me, anyway."

"What is it like, then?" Ewan said softly. "Tell me, Clare."

"Oh, I can't—how do you think *I* know? You seem to have it all worked out, Ewan! How did *you* find out?"

"Oh, well, I *have* many married friends, and I do see films and plays, and try to keep up with modern trends outside my safe, secure bachelor existence, and it sometimes strikes me that I'm missing so much."

"You?"

"Don't sound so shocked and incredulous! Why not me? Am I such a crusty individual, bound up with my books and my work, that you can't see me any more as a human being? That's a sad commentary on the way I've been slipping, Clare. I wonder if I've slipped too far to pull myself back to where it would be possible to start again? Attain the things I've missed?"

"I think you've been hiding your gift for acting, all this time, Ewan," Clare said, recovered now. "If I didn't know you as well as I do, I'd think of you as the poor man on the outside, looking in—you know the chap, watching the people eating, while he was outside in the cold?"

"Don't laugh, Clare. It isn't really funny at all," he said quietly, closing his hand over hers and not caring about anyone else beyond the radius of their table. The waiter was hovering, waiting to put the menu in front of them, but like Mrs. Hewitt at the table not too far away from them, he assumed that these two people didn't want food at the moment. Something else was of far more importance to them.

"I feel like that man, Clare," Ewan said. "Only I'm looking in the window at you; it's you, not food, that I'm . . . hungry for."

7

CLARE suddenly pulled herself together. This was going altogether too far.

"Ewan, you're overdoing it!" she said.

He looked shocked for a moment, then with a smile he sat back.

The spell was broken. The waiter, hovering near, brought the menu, and conversation was normal again.

Clare felt rather shaken. Out of the corner of her eye she could see that Ewan's friends were looking across at them occasionally, with more interest than she cared about. Mrs. Hewitt didn't look as happy as when she had at first come in.

Clare began to wish she hadn't taken this job on. When they were alone again, she said tentatively, "Ewan, what do you propose to do now? I mean, you've rather over-acted, haven't you? Surely you haven't convinced your friends?"

He smiled. "Oh, I think I have! I doubt if we shall get out of here tonight without a pressing invitation from her. She'll want to see how friendly we are, and re-arrange the battle accordingly. We mustn't underestimate Mrs. Hewitt's tactics."

She fingered the pearl necklace nervously.

"What are you worried about, Clare?"

"I'm afraid you'll commit me too far for me to ever get out again."

"But you said there was no one else in your life to complicate things, Clare."

"But there might be," she said defensively. "I did tell you, didn't I, that I was willing, so long as I could get out again?"

He looked put out for a moment, but quickly recovered. "My dear Clare, as I reminded you before, an engagement can be broken. We shall be officially engaged in due course, but you can give me back the ring later."

His low tones made the thing sound so intimate that she shifted her shoulders restlessly. "What good will that do? If as you seem to think, my being engaged to you will keep Mrs. Hewitt away, what will happen when I break it off?"

"If you can last out long enough, she will have taken her daughter off on the inevitable cruise, and there found another man with all the advantages she seems to think I have!" he retorted, and it struck Clare that he didn't seem very pleased about something.

"Oh, very well, I'll stop worrying about it," she said, and flashed her brilliant smile at him.

"Clare, let's——" he began, then abruptly stopped, as the waiter reappeared at his elbow.

Dancing began. It was a very good orchestra, and Ewan asked her to dance. She hadn't expected that. Somehow he seemed the sort of man to keep aloof from such pleasures, but his height and good balance gave him a distinction on the dance floor that surprised her.

Mrs. Hewitt seized her chance to send over one of the men from her party to ask Clare for the next dance, but she caught Ewan's frown, so she refused. "I'm one of those awful people who don't really like letting my food cool while I'm dancing," she said, with a special smile for the disappointed young man.

He bowed and went back to Mrs. Hewitt, and Ewan smiled grimly. "Oh,

147

dear, I think we'd better go soon, Clare. How would you like a drive, and some supper at a smaller place later?"

Clare was so pleased to get out of that hotel that she turned and waved gaily at Mrs. Hewitt's party as they left. She hoped that Ewan wouldn't become embarrassingly intense when she was alone with him, but anything would be better than this.

Ewan, however, was his old cool self again. He drove along the coast, chatting easily, and when they had supper he outlined what he hoped she would be able to do until they were officially engaged.

It sounded a reasonable programme. No more than two evenings out per week. She was relieved.

They stayed talking so long that it was late when she reached home. The house was in darkness, so it looked as if the children had settled down all right and Alison was in bed.

Clare let herself in quietly, and took off the necklace, standing there in the hall. For her general peace of mind, she decided not to show it to Alison just yet. She would have enough to worry about, as it was, without starting a lot of questions at home.

She crept upstairs, and paused outside Jayne's room. There was a low-burning light on the landing. She could see that Jayne, at least, was fast asleep, the bed in its usual ruffled state, Jayne's idea of being comfortable being to get the blankets pulled up in a bundle, and her bare arms flung over the side of the bed.

Clare passed on to Susan's room, where Mellie's cot was. The door was shut, for some reason. It was a trying door, and squeaked, so Clare decided to leave it alone. Perhaps Alison considered there was a draught with the door open.

Alison was already in bed. Her door was ajar, presumably to permit her to hear any sounds from the children. Clare hoped she wouldn't wake her sister.

She decided to take her night things into the bathroom to undress, so as not to disturb Alison.

When she came back in her pyjamas, she heard a sound, rather like soft hiccoughing, or crying. Jayne? Mellie? She tiptoed to both doors and listened. It certainly wasn't Jayne. Mellie was restless, but the sounds weren't coming from there.

Astonished, she went back to her own room and stood by Alison's bed. Alison had the blankets pulled over her head, and she must have been holding her breath until Clare moved away.

At last she couldn't stand it any longer, and went and sat on the side of her sister's bed.

"Alison! What on earth's wrong, darling?" she asked urgently, putting her hand on Alison's shoulder.

Alison shrugged her off. "Oh, leave me alone!" she stormed. "Just leave me alone!"

"Alison! That isn't like you! What is it? Are you ill? Is Mellie worse?" Clare asked, as it struck her that something might have gone wrong while she had been out.

"No, no, the children are all right," Alison sobbed, and buried her face in the pillow. "If you must know, I'm tired and I just can't get to sleep!"

It seemed a very unfamiliar thing for Alison of all people to make a fuss about, so Clare got up and went to her own bed.

"Are you sure you wouldn't like a hot

drink or something?" she asked, making one last effort.

"Yes, but I'll get it myself," Alison said and swung her legs out of bed.

Clare listened puzzled, to Alison's soft padding footsteps hurrying down the stairs.

She couldn't rest without knowing what was wrong. She went quietly down after her, and found Alison standing leaning against the kitchen window frame, her hot face against the glass. There was mist where her hot cheeks had touched the cold surface. Her face was flushed and her eyes swollen.

"Is it because I went out so suddenly?" Clare persisted. "Well, it isn't *like* you to be like this!"

"How do you know what I'm like?" Alison asked, unaccountably. "That's right, you look all surprised and injured. Why didn't you *tell* me about Ewan Burnett?"

"What about him?" Clare asked carefully.

"Pretending it was just a working afternoon yesterday. Pretending it wasn't all arranged tonight! I would much rather you had told me you were on the point of being engaged to him! Anyway, it doesn't matter."

"How did you know about all that?" Clare asked carefully, wondering what could have happened to make Alison so upset about the knowledge anyway.

"Someone telephoned, about nine thirty. She said you'd been dining at the Three Drovers and after you'd gone, she saw you'd left something behind."

"Who rang up? Did she say what her name was?" Clare asked incredulously.

"Hewitt, I think. Double name. Mrs. Something-or-other Hewitt."

"Mrs. Lattimore Hewitt?"

"Yes. You know her, then?"

"I met her, tonight. Oh, what a mess! She might at least have let me get home first. What did she say?"

"She said she wondered if you'd arrived home and whether she'd have to congratulate you tonight. Clare, it doesn't matter to me if you sit holding hands with someone across a table—I don't care what you do! But for pity's sake let me know what's going on so that I won't seem a complete ass when someone rings up like that."

"But you're not all upset just because some silly old woman jumps to conclusions and makes an excuse to ring up and find out if she's right, are you, Alison? It's only one of Ewan's friends, and she's just nosy, that's all."

"The children told me it was Ewan you were keen on. You could have told me, when I first arrived."

"The children? Well, I don't know what gave them that impression!"

"It's no use being angry with them, Clare. It was something they heard you say to Susan that made them say it."

"But I never mentioned him to Susan!" Clare exploded. "Oh, wait a bit—yes, I did. What was it I said?"

"It doesn't matter, Clare!"

"But it does! What did those children hear that they've gossiped about? Goodness, they might have told the doctor even!"

"Would it have mattered?" Alison asked quietly.

Clare eyed her sister. No, of course it

wouldn't matter. Alison was telling her that the doctor was hers already.

"What time did he go, Alison?" she asked, abandoning the subject of Ewan and what she had said to Susan about him.

"He stayed on a bit, till I'd got Jayne to bed. He was anxious about Mellie. Then he went."

She turned and purposefully got her milk out of the fridge and took it upstairs with her.

At the bend of the stairs she paused. "I saw you get out of his car. You had a necklace on. Is it new?"

"Yes. Tonight. I thought you'd be asleep, so I didn't bother about it. Would you like to see it?"

She thought Alison was going to refuse, but she nodded her head and sat on the stairs. "Bring it here—I don't want to put the light on in the bedroom. It might wake Jayne up."

Clare crept quietly into her room and using a torch, found the pearl necklace where she had carelessly thrown it among the things on her dressing-table.

When she took it back to Alison, there

was a startled silence, then Alison said: "But this is gorgeous!"

"Rather nice, isn't it?" she said. She wanted to tell Alison all about it, how she had insisted it should be returnable at the end of this ridiculous deception, this make-believe engagement that was about to become an established fact at any time. But she was really under a bond of secrecy although Ewan hadn't actually sworn her to it.

While she hesitated, Alison said, in an aloof little voice, "So what that woman said was true! You are on the point of becoming engaged to him! How long did you think you could keep it a secret—or is everyone supposed to know but me?"

"Alison! This isn't *like* you! I was going to tell you, but I thought you'd be tired out after today! And believe me, it wasn't planned! It just happened!"

"You had no idea he was going to propose tonight?"

"But he didn't!" Clare protested. "I expect he will, soon—he hinted he might —but tonight he was just, well, telling me how much he liked me and that he didn't want to stay a bachelor for ever—until that beastly old woman came along, and she kept staring at us all the time!"

"Well, it's all very peculiar," Alison said, finishing her milk and getting up.

"What did she think I'd left behind?" Clare asked suddenly, thinking.

"Your gloves," Alison threw over her shoulder, as she went into the bedroom.

"These are the gloves I had with me," Clare said quietly, picking them up off the dressing-table. "So that rather proves she only rang up to find out something, doesn't it?"

"All right, Clare, you've made your point," Alison said wearily.

"But you weren't crying just because I hadn't told you about this, *I* know!" Clare said shrewdly. "Something happened tonight, didn't it? Something else, I mean? Something while Raymond Shaw was here!"

"No, he'd gone already—" Alison blurted out.

"So something did happen! Honey, why won't you *tell* me?"

"Oh, leave me *alone!*" Alison stormed, jumping into bed again.

Clare decided not to do anything else

about it that night. A little later on she heard Alison's deep regular breathing, and then she dropped off to sleep herself.

Mellie was still sleeping when Clare was ready to start out for the surgery next morning, but Jayne was up.

She was sitting disconsolately at the table glaring at a boiled egg, when Clare rushed downstairs, late.

"What's the matter, sweetie?" Clare asked, pausing to look at the child.

"I hate boiled eggs what isn't hats-off!" Jayne muttered.

"I'll take his hat off for you if you like," Clare offered.

"No, don't you bother," Alison said, coming in at that moment with the tray of tea-things. "Here, give it to me, Jayne! I had to rush out without doing it because the kettle started whistling. I don't want Mellie wakened yet."

She expertly sliced off the top of the egg, peppered and salted it, and set the spoon in the child's hand, cut up fingers of bread and butter ready for "dipping" and poured tea for Clare and herself; smoothly, with the precision of long habit. She looks serene and lovely, a typical

157

young mother, Clare thought. Why did that tiresome Keith Everton want to upset her? He should have married her quickly, before someone like Dr. Shaw came along.

"The telephone kept ringing last night," Jayne said. She was in a complaining mood this morning. She kept it up in a sad monotone, and she looked frankly surly.

"No, darling," Alison said quickly, looking anxious. "It just rang when someone called to know where Clare was."

"It kept ringing," Jayne repeated. "It waked me up."

"No, you only thought it did, darling," Alison urged, pouring milk in Jayne's mug and holding it to the child's lips.

"You were shouting at someone!" Jayne offered.

Alison looked bothered, but contented herself with shaking her head at the child.

"And you was crying," Jayne insisted, her grammar going to the winds in her earnestness to make her point and be believed.

"Oh, Jayne, how can you?" Alison cried.

"I heard you!" Jayne repeated. "It was someone called *Keef*."

"Oh, these children!" Alison said, in exasperation, getting up and dashing out to the kitchen.

Clare got up to go. So that was it! Keith Everton had rung up last night and upset Alison.

She hadn't time to take it up with her sister then, but she resolved to speak to her about it later.

She felt she would give the world to find out the truth of that strange business. She didn't believe in her heart that Keith Everton had fallen for someone because she was more pretty than Alison. No, it was something else. Alison had been oddly evasive, and made a lot out of this business of seeing the medical student in Keith's car with him, when she had first arrived in Rexmundham. It had seemed at the time rather too thin a story to break up a pair like Keith and Alison, who had been so much in love.

Clare caught the district nurse up half way up the street, and got a lift to the surgery. She would have been very late if she hadn't had that bit of luck.

"How are you getting on with your other job up at Wycherley Holt, dear?"

Miss Quinney asked. She was fat and cheerful and rather garrulous.

"Oh, all right, thanks," Clare said; and she was at a loss to know whether Ewan might be glad if she were to broadcast by this easy means the fact that he was no longer free for Mrs. Lattimore Hewitt's future plans, or whether she should preserve a discreet silence.

But Miss Quinney had already heard. "Oh, I should have thought you'd have said you were getting on marvellously, dear," she said, with an arch smile. "I was called in to old Mrs. Tanner late last night (you know, at Bickers' End) and she said, between wheezes, that her daughter (whose husband is a waiter at The Three Drovers in Illingfold if you remember) said he saw you and Mr. Burnett with *eyes for no one else but each other*, and a certain person who had better not be mentioned was absolutely red with rage at a nearby table, her having designs on him for her daughter, if you know who I mean!"

"Oh, this place!" Clare exploded. "How come you were called in last night to the waiter's mother-in-law?"

160

"Fate, dear. I believe in it. I said to Dr. Shaw, well, you'll have to pull your socks up, my lad, and start thinking of looking for a new morning secretary! I only said it as a joke, but he didn't seem to like it."

"Oh, no! Don't tell me he was there last night too!" Clare cried.

"Well, you know old Mrs. Tanner—she will call him in for the least thing!" Miss Quinney said, with satisfaction. "Mind you, I've known Raymond Shaw since he was a nipper. A nice lad—I've always liked him—but I always say the girl who gets him will have a handful, with those moods of his. Still, come to think of it, I wouldn't mind being a girl, taking on the job myself!" she finished, laughing.

8

THE District Nurse dropped Clare outside the doctor's house. "Go easy with him this morning, dear—he had a very bad night. He won't be in a good temper!"

Clare smiled briefly at Miss Quinney. "I'll remember, and thanks for the lift," and she flashed into the side gate and up the path.

She just got in and changed into her white coat in time to open the waiting-room door.

It was a full house this morning. Plenty of coughs and colds and wheezing. There was a badly cut thumb in one corner, which Clare was about to have into the surgery at once, over the heads of those who had been waiting, when she noticed little Miss Lupton waiting patiently. She was a heart case and usually was allowed in first.

Miss Lupton looked at the blood-stained bandage and said in a frightened voice,

"Take him in first, dear. I'll wait a little."

Clare took the lad into the surgery. Raymond looked up briefly, saw the blood and the white face, nodded, and they got started on him. Clare felt an unreasonable gratitude to that full and urgent waiting-room this morning. At least it put off any questions about Ewan.

The morning ripped by. Between the telephone, the appointments pad, the filing cabinet, and the patients, Clare had hardly time to look at the doctor, which was as well, for he was in no mood to be smiling and pleasant this morning.

"That poor Sims' child!" he exploded. "I shall have her admitted to hospital, I think! She can do no worse than she is at home!"

His father came in at that moment, and they had an altercation about the little Sims' girl, while Clare was trying to coax a big boy in; a boy who had sat stolidly almost an hour in the waiting-room, and now panicked. His mother did nothing to help.

Raymond Shaw appeared at the door and said crisply, "Where is the next

163

patient?" He didn't like being kept waiting.

He quickly took in the situation, fixed the boy with an eye, and said, "Come along in, old chap—I've no time to waste this morning!" and the boy shambled to his feet.

At that moment—the most unfortunate moment that could have been chosen that morning—the latest arrival fussily sat herself in the seat the boy had vacated and said to Clare in a loud high carrying voice, "Oh, there you are, Miss Drury! Didn't expect to see you at work this morning, after what they're saying in the town about you and Mr. Burnett!"

It electrified the atmosphere. Everyone looked at Clare, and those who had been making a pretence of reading the tired-looking magazines on the central table, put them down to watch what was going on.

Briefly Clare and the doctor exchanged glances, then Raymond Shaw said crisply, "You'd better shut the outer door, I think. It's ten minutes early, but I'll never get through by lunch-time at this rate."

This produced the usual odd couple of patients who got to their feet, mumbling that their cases weren't so important and could wait till the next day. It even caused the last arrival to retire into abashed silence, but the moment Clare had shut the door and followed the doctor and the boy into the surgery, she heard the woman say, "I didn't know the doctor was out here— who'd have expected him to be? But it's true, you know—what they're saying in the town about her and that Ewan Burnett!" and there followed a great deal of whispering.

Whispering, indistinct conversations, the low mumble of things said beyond that surgery door, were always rather frustrating, but none more so than today, when it concerned Clare so personally. She was conscious, too, in the doctor's downbent head—as he peered into the boy's throat and up his nostrils—of irritation, disapproval, an impatience to take it up with her, find out what it was all about.

When surgery finished at last, the telephone rang again. Clare had been getting for him his list of routine calls, and the pad of notes about new calls. This was another urgent one, up at Foxgate Farm.

"That old boiler-house! Another burns case—I'll have to go there first," Raymond said. "When will they learn? I've told them till I'm tired, that that old boiler is a menace!"

He got his bag, took off his white coat while he was reading his notes, quickly checked that everything was ready for him (although he had seen Clare doing it) and as an afterthought called out to his father.

Clare began to get ready for a session of note-making at the big desk, and she was surprised when the doctor came back and said, "Come on, get your coat on, Clare!"

"Where am I going?" she asked in surprise.

"With me, of course! I can't ever get time for a word with you in surgery so we'll have to talk on the way. You might be able to help me on my rounds today, anyway."

Her heart sank. She wasn't going to get out of being questioned about Ewan, she could see.

He took the big black car today. He had once said laughingly that the patients were more reassured if the doctor arrived in a sober looking vehicle than one with a convertible hood that looked as if it had been made for fun.

Foxgate Farm was over Farthing Bridge way. They had to go through Rexmundham. Clare looked unseeingly at the shops and the quaint streets of the town, and wondered how Raymond Shaw would begin.

As soon as he got through the last lot of traffic lights, he said, "That old gossip Quinney is on about you and Burnett! Any truth in it?"

So that was it! If Miss Quinney hadn't told him, he might not have known. It was doubtful if the patient had offered the information to the doctor.

"What did she say?" Clare said carefully.

"Oh, for heaven's sake, Clare—is there any truth in it, or isn't there? I heard you myself making arrangements to go out to dinner with him last night. Why didn't you say it was in the wind?"

He always used colloquialisms when he was ruffled. She said, "Because I didn't know he was going to suggest it."

"Now look, Clare—according to Miss Quinney, you're practically engaged to the chap! According to Alison, you reluctantly went out for a working afternoon with him to some castle, and that was all. Now, which *is* the truth?"

"Why are you asking me? It won't affect my work in the surgery."

"Are you inviting me to mind my own business, Clare?" he asked, and his voice fairly crackled with ice.

She sighed. "No, you know me better than that! What I don't understand is, why you have changed so much lately. Nothing I can do pleases you, yet I do my best in the surgery, and I have offered, time and time again, to work for you outside surgery hours, help you in any way you care to name. Well, you didn't want extra help from me, so I got another spare time job. You know all this. I've made no secret of it from the first."

"But they're saying you're on the point of being engaged to the fellow!" he exploded.

"Then they're saying more than he is," she couldn't help retorting. "If it looks as if he is getting more than friendly with me, what does it matter to anyone else? It isn't as if there were anyone else who cared about me! I'm free as air, and I've made no secret of it. If this has come as a surprise to other people, I can only say that it has all happened rather suddenly, too suddenly for me to have the chance to tell anyone about it, even if I had wanted to."

"What's happened rather suddenly?"

"Me being seen out with Ewan Burnett," she explained patiently.

He was silent while he took his turn in a line of vehicles crawling in snake-like procession through the narrow opening between road works and cement mixers, then he returned to the attack, but he was quieter now. None the less purposeful, however.

"It's just because I feel responsible for you, Clare. You're my secretary. I've warned you about Burnett. He isn't the sort of chap you should be around with, getting very friendly with his sort."

"What *do* you mean?"

"You know what I mean, Clare, but you won't take it in. I suppose this is why you were so odd yesterday when we went up the hill to look at the view—you knew you were going to be so friendly with him very soon that people would start talking."

"Really, Dr. Shaw!"

"It was Raymond yesterday, remember?"

"That was when we were out together with the children, on a picnic—it would have been awful to remain formal. But we're at work at the moment."

"I see. Well, if that's the way you want it!" He thought about it some more, then he burst out, "Why didn't you say honestly that you'd been out with Burnett on the Saturday? As I remember it, you said vaguely that you'd been out with 'someone'. Why make a mystery of it, if you didn't know how things were going to shape up?"

"Perhaps it was because you were using a rather hectoring tone," she said, "and I probably just didn't feel like it. I didn't really see how it could concern anyone else."

They left the main road for a secondary road where the houses grew steadily more scarce until the cart-track came into view —the one entrance up to Foxgate Farm.

He had a great deal to say about the

state of it, but with good reason. He had to slow down to walking pace, so that his tyres weren't ripped to ribbons. "This family really deserves everything that comes to it!" she heard him mutter. "For sheer inefficiency and cheeseparing ways, they really are the end! Something awful will happen one day, and they can't say I haven't warned them."

At the top of the track, a lad waited, swinging idly on a five-barred gate. He was detailed to show them where to leave the car, and to guide them to one of the many entrances to the farmhouse.

It was old, but it had no attractions whatever. The ceilings were low, but not beamed. The wallpaper was faded, tired, without being dirty or peeling. Everything was just about adequate and dreadfully dreary, and it had the air of an unloved house.

The patient was the farmer's second son, Percy. He was in a great deal of pain.

After a brief examination, Raymond Shaw asked them what they thought they were doing. "He should have been sent to hospital—why didn't you call for the ambulance?"

"You're doing all right, doc, aren't you?" the farmer said, grinning. "You're our doctor. What do we want with strangers at the hospital for? Besides, they'd want to bed him, and he's got work to do."

"You'll have to bed him anyway," Raymond Shaw said, doing the best he could. "I'm not sure he won't have to go to hospital, anyway. I'll ring them."

"Now see here, doc, he's the only one who understands the boiler. You can't take him off us, not just now! We haven't got enough pairs of hands as it is!"

"Then get some more!" He looked round for a telephone. "And he can't do anything until he's fit. And perhaps you'll get a new boiler now this has happened!"

"Yes, well, it's not as simple as all that," the farmer whined. "We've had a bad year and we don't understand new-fangled things, and there's the pit to be finished digging, and the barn to be shored up, and there's lambing and—"

"And there's the little matter of your sons' lives," the doctor sharply reminded him. "You'll count money against them too often, you mark my words!"

He talked again into the receiver, and finally hung up. "I've sent for the ambulance, and see you don't obstruct them in getting him away quickly."

The farmer looked in amazement at his son. "He's making a bit of a fuss, isn't he? Don't you think you can lay up for weeks in hospital, son, and leave yon boiler to your brothers—they're no good at it!"

"He's in a great deal of pain," the doctor said, slowly and with emphasis. "I've done the best I can for him, but some of those burns are deep-seated. Oh, you wouldn't understand! Where's his mother?"

"Milking," the farmer said, in a surly voice. "And don't go wasting her time, neither. We're all behind as it is."

The farm buildings all needed repair. Raymond Shaw looked at them in disgust when they at last left the farm. "He's got plenty of money. I happen to know, the old skinflint. As if he can't get all this put right. Making his wife work like that! Won't pay the hands enough money to keep them here, that's what it is!"

They didn't return the same way to Rexmundham, but took in other patients

173

in a wide circle. Clare hoped Raymond would be too angry with the people at Foxgate Farm, to remember to come back to his quarrel with her, but he wasn't. He remembered it while they were waiting at the level crossing for the London train to go through.

"Clare, if Burnett asks you to marry him, are you going to?"

"I'll tell you in good time to get someone to take my place," she said, after drawing a deep breath.

"Then you *are* going to marry him?"

"I expect so," she was driven to say.

"You can't do! Clare, you don't know enough about him!"

"And you've made vague hints about him and you refused to tell me anything. I don't believe you know anything about him to his discredit. You just don't like him and you've been listening to rumours!"

"That's not true, Clare!"

"Well, you listened to old Miss Quinney's gossiping about me, and didn't even ask me if it was true!"

"I heard one of the patients talking about it this morning, in my own waiting-room, remember?" he retorted. "And if it's facts you want, I can tell you here and now that I've heard he made his money in a very odd way."

"He inherited it, from his father!" she corrected him sharply.

"Then his father made it in a way that wouldn't do for a lot of people in this town! Why else do you think no one invites him to their homes?"

"It could be that they have, and he hasn't been willing to go to their homes. Patronising lot!"

"It's no use getting heated and making stupid remarks like that, Clare! He'd like to be accepted by the best families—"

"Oh, Dr. Shaw, do stop this silly line of reasoning," she begged. "There are many mothers of young daughters only too willing to get their hands on his money by marriage. I've seen at least one of them campaigning for a rich husband for her child."

"I'm not disputing that, but I am disputing that this person is any better than he is. She won't be one of the best people in this town, I know—no one will have him. Not those who know how the money was made, anyway."

"Well, *how* was his money made? And what else have you got against him?"

But her question wasn't answered; for they had arrived at another patient's house.

He left her in the car while he went in. She sat seething. If it were anyone else, she would have said that this stupid line of argument had been promoted by sheer jealousy, but that, of course, could not be the case with the doctor. Besides, it was pretty plain that he was fond of Alison, to the exclusion of all else.

There were only two more new cases to see and then, she promised herself, she would tackle him about the rumours. She couldn't go through with this thing if there were really any truth in what he was alleging, and much as she was angry with the doctor, she knew better than to think he was just trading on rumours without foundation. On the other hand, if he had been misinformed, she must, for her own sake, put it all right. She couldn't be engaged to a man that the whole district was insinuating things about.

He had simmered down by the time he came out of the patient's house, and he looked at her in a propitiating manner as he sat behind the wheel and put his bag in the back seat.

"Clare, don't let's fight," he almost pleaded.

"Well, who started fighting? I'm willing not to," she laughed.

"Good. And do you have to be so friendly with Burnett? You know I wouldn't say things about anyone without some foundation of truth. Why, good heavens, even in that dignified family I have just been visiting, there was the odd word flung against him."

"Yes, but what did they *say*?"

"Well, they didn't call him a bounder exactly, but they did say they wished Wycherley Holt hadn't been bought and occupied by that man!"

Clare felt uneasy. She had to admit that at first she hadn't really liked Ewan Burnett all that much herself. There was just *something*, hard to put into words but there all the same, which she hadn't quite liked or understood.

"I wonder if Alison had heard something?" she murmured, half to herself. "She didn't like the idea either."

"You told your sister? When? She didn't tell me anything about it!"

"Oh, yes, what happened last night?" Clare turned round on him. "When I came home, she was very upset. She was crying, and she tried to have me think she was worried about me. Then it came out this morning that her ex-fiancé had rung her up. Were you still in the house then?"

"No. No, I'd gone not long after you went. She had no telephone calls while I was there." He looked anxious, but not unduly put out, Clare thought, as she watched him closely.

"Well, don't you *mind*, that someone upset her?" she said at last. "Doesn't it mean anything that her former fiancé has been on the telephone to her?"

"I think you're determined to quarrel with me, Clare," he said, after a significant pause. "I imagine she can handle that young man perfectly well, and I don't believe she'd cry over him, from what I've heard about him," he said stiffly, as he started up the car and drove out into the mainstream of traffic.

"By the way," he said, a little later, "how is Mellie this morning?"

"I wondered when you were going to ask," Clare commented.

"Well, she was all right when I left her last night. She's a healthy little rascal, and she was treated pretty quickly after her ducking, not only by a doctor but a trained children's nurse!" he retorted. "There is a little matter, too, of a rather hectic morning, which you haven't helped, which has all put it out of my head, but if she'd been ill last night, I'd have remembered. I'd have called in on my way home from an all-night call."

Rub it in, she thought. "Yes, I heard about that call from Miss Quinney when she gave me a lift this morning," she said coolly. "And I agree, you don't have to worry about Mellie. She was still asleep when I came out, and Alison's wonderful with children."

"Yes, she certainly is," he agreed, warmth flooding his voice. "She ought to be looking after children of her own."

And if I didn't really believe which way his thoughts were going, she told herself bitterly, then that just about confirms it!

"I suppose you'll look in, then, when you drop me at Susan's house?"

"I wasn't going to," he said, looking straight ahead.

"Don't you want to see Alison?"

"In your present mood I suppose you'll go and tell her I didn't want to see her, if I say no?" he said, turning to face Clare.

"My mood! Honestly, I don't understand you! Never mind! Let's forget the whole thing!"

"Yes, let's," he agreed.

In a wretched silence, they drove the rest of the way to Susan's house.

Clare gathered her things and was going to hurry in, when he held her by the arm. "Clare, I know you'll say it's none of my business—" he began, when Alison ran down the path, and looked in at the open window his side.

"Oh, there you are, Raymond!" she gasped. "I've been phoning the surgery since you went out—I must have just missed you!"

"What's wrong?" he asked sharply, opening his door and getting out at once, Clare forgotten.

"It's Mellie!" Alison gasped.

9

CLARE got out of the car, but the doctor had already reached in for his bag and was following Alison up the path.

Clare caught snatches of what they were saying. ". . . and she seemed rather white and feverish and when I took her temperature . . ."

". . . how long has she been like this?"

". . . a pain in her chest, and she isn't making a noise—that isn't like Mellie when she isn't well . . ."

Their heads were together, and Clare didn't catch them up until they had reached the stairs.

"Is there anything I can do?" she asked her sister.

Alison turned a distraught face to Clare as if she had forgotten her existence.

"Yes, you can keep Jayne quiet, if you will," Alison said, with a little rush. "She was at the kitchen sink when I last telephoned Raymond."

Clare found Jayne drenched but happy, trying to make the next door kitten swim in the washing-up bowl.

Clare rescued the kitten, stuffed Jayne's open mouth (as she prepared to bawl on a top note in sheer anger and disappointment at losing her new game) with a chocolate, and started to strip off her wet clothes.

"What an unkind thing to do to that poor little thing!" she scolded, as she worked. "Look at him. We must find him a towel and roll him up in it, in front of the fire!"

"Mrs. Wheeler doesn't want him," Jayne said, with conviction. "She wouldn't mind me teaching him to swim!"

"How do you know that? She'll be very angry when I put him back over the fence!"

She wrapped a big towel round Jayne's naked and rather shivery young body, and found a kitchen cloth to mop the worst off the kitten, then she gave it some warm milk. "It's only a tiny little baby cat! How could you, Jayne!"

"Mrs. Wheeler was teaching the other kittens to swim," Jayne said with brooding eyes. "She held them under, so I did, too."

Clare's eyes widened, as she realised what the child had seen. "Oh, did she! Well, we'll have to see about that, won't we. Oh, what a mess! Do you think you could be very, very quiet while poor Mellie is so poorly?"

"She stuffed herself with sweets from Mummy's drawer because she was hungry," Jayne said. "She'll prob'bly be sick. I hope she is!"

"You little horror! Come on upstairs and let's find you some more clothes."

She hadn't a lot of time before she was due to be at Ewan Burnett's house, so she whipped up a quick omelette and settled Jayne beside her to share it, for on this most peculiar of mornings, Alison didn't appear to have started lunch. The cold empty oven struck Clare as the strangest thing.

She opened a can of fruit, and they had some and were busy with a glass of cold milk apiece when Alison and the doctor came downstairs.

Alison looked relieved to see that Jayne was being fed. "Oh, good! I'm afraid I haven't had a chance to think of food. Oh, I suppose you'll have to go up to Wycherley Holt, Clare!"

"There *is* a lot to do, but I suppose I could telephone and get today off," Clare said doubtfully. "Do you need me here, Alison?"

Alison glanced at Raymond Shaw.

"Of course Clare will stay with you this afternoon, won't you, Clare?" he said, and he sounded rather surprised that Clare should even consider going to work. But then, of course, he didn't like her going to work for Ewan Burnett at any time, she reminded herself.

"I'll see what I can do," Clare promised. "What's wrong with Mellie, anyway?"

"I don't know yet," Raymond said rather crossly. "It's that rash I don't like," he said to Alison.

They went out to the car, both talking quietly. Then Alison stood nodding, taking instructions.

Ewan sounded rather cross too, when Clare finally got him to answer the telephone.

"How tiresome, Clare! There's so much to do! But you'll be able to come up this evening, won't you? I'll call and pick you up!"

"Can I let you know later?" Clare pleaded. "My sister is rather young to be left with a sick child."

"She's a trained nurse, isn't she?"

He sounded so heartless. He would have made a better impression on her if he had given her the time off without question. He must have known she would make it up to him.

"I will come into work if you can't manage without me," she answered.

"Now, Clare, don't be so frigid with me! I'm worried, my dear. I have a dead-line with my publishers, you know that; a deadline I looked to you, trusted you to help me keep."

"I'll come this afternoon, then," she said.

"No, wait! Clare! All right, I know if you come, you'll be too anxious to work. You'd better stay at home until tomorrow, then."

She replaced the receiver and stood thinking. There had been no warmth in his voice. What had happened to the excitement, that disturbing excitement, that had taken possession of him, sitting at the table in The Three Drovers last night? He had acted like a man in love. Acted . . . was that all it was? If so, then he had a hidden talent that might be dangerous.

Already he was being possessive. It followed that she would be engaged to him soon. If he wanted to continue right through to marriage, for the sake of defending himself from fluffy young women, and providing himself with a secretary into the bargain, what would she say? She supposed she had better make up her mind fairly soon, but the thought of being married to him struck her at this moment as being rather like caught in a trap. Where was she going? All her instincts rose against him, because he hadn't shown any consideration for a child's illness or for her own anxiety to stay at home and help.

Alison came into the house. The roar of the doctor's car lessened and faded into the distance, and with the silence that followed it, Clare felt an aching loneliness. Even when she was sparring with him, Raymond Shaw gave her a comfort and solidity that was hard to beat, and prone to be missed when he wasn't there.

"What's happening, Clare? Are you going to Wycherley Holt this afternoon?"

"No. I'm to stay here until tomorrow."

"Oh, how kind of Mr. Burnett!" Alison said warmly. "I told Raymond he would release you for this afternoon, but Raymond said he wouldn't—or if he did, he'd want you to work tonight. Raymond doesn't like your Mr. Burnett, does he?"

"No, I don't think he does," Clare agreed.

"You don't look very pleased about it. What upset you, Clare?"

"Oh, nothing. Alison, what about Mellie? Don't you know what's wrong with her?"

Alison shook her head, and listened. "She's trying to call me—I'll just run upstairs—"

Clare followed her up, then wondered what had happened to Jayne. She had left her sitting at the table, she remembered.

She couldn't find her. Alison came down presently, and asked where the child was.

"She must be hiding," Clare said, frowning. "Where would she be?"

"Oh, Clare, we must keep an eye on that child! She keeps trying to get next door, to play with young Billy. I don't want measles to complicate everything!"

"Measles! It wouldn't be measles, would it?"

Alison smiled briefly. "No, it wouldn't. Nothing so easy."

Her fleeting smile vanished, and she muttered: "I wish it was."

"Well, don't worry, it's probably only a tummy upset. I don't suppose all those chocolates did her any good."

"What chocolates?"

Clare repeated Jayne's conversation, which led her to the episode of the kitten. "That's where she'll be—with that kitten!" and she ran out to the kitchen. The back door was open, and neither Jayne nor the kitten were to be seen.

"Clare, come back!" Alison called. "Tell me about the chocolates. Where did the children get them? Susan doesn't eat chocolates—she told me, because I was going to get her some for the journey. She doesn't eat sweets at all. You must know that!"

"Yes, of course! How stupid of me.

188

Well, it was something out of Susan's drawer that Mellie ate." They exchanged glances, and Clare said, "For goodness' sake go up and look, while I search for Jayne. We must question her more—she might have had some herself."

Clare found Jayne in the next garden, chasing a puppy. "He made the kitten go in that hole and he won't leave it alone!" she stormed.

"All right, I'll get it out, but you must go back to the house. It's too cold to be out here."

Alison was in the kitchen, standing worriedly looking at a small box that had held the chocolates. "It must have been a gift to Susan and she hadn't eaten any. Well, they've all gone. They looked pretty sophisticated for a three-year-old, I must say! I'd better tell Raymond."

"No, wait a minute. Let's ask Jayne some more about it. Did you eat any, Jayne?"

Jayne stuck her lip out and looked sulky.

"Listen, darling," Alison coaxed, and went down on her knees beside Jayne. "Mellie's been horribly sick. Perhaps she'll be better now, but if we'd known before, we could have made her well sooner. Now, you don't want to be ill, do you?"

Jayne looked frightened for a moment, then she straddled her legs out wide, thrust her hands into the pockets of her trousers, and said, "Shan't be ill. Not me!"

"Then you didn't eat any?"

Clare said irritably, "Let's not waste any more time, Alison. If she won't tell us, she won't. Dr. Shaw will give her something to make her sick, just in case."

"No, don't do that, Clare!" Alison protested. "That isn't the way. Jayne, darling, did you eat Mummy's chocolates?"

Jayne thought about it and said clearly, "No, I didn't eat Mummy's chocolates."

Alison got up and went to the telephone. "Well, so now we know. Mellie had them and Jayne didn't. Mellie should get over it pretty soon now."

Jayne watched her thoughtfully. She listened to Alison talking to the doctor, and she waited patiently while Alison went upstairs and took Mellie's temperature,

190

then she sat down in the middle of the floor and scowled.

"Now what's the matter with this child?" Clare murmured to Alison.

"I don't know, but now I really feel I can relax, but I just wish I knew more about those chocolates, as Susan never eats them. There's something wrong somewhere. I don't know. You'd think Sue would have given them to someone who did, rather than put them in her stocking drawer—it isn't like her."

"I expect she was in such a turmoil of excitement getting away on that trip that she just didn't know what she *was* doing."

"Speak to Mummy on the telephone and ask her," Jayne said suddenly.

"Don't be silly, darling. Mummy and Daddy are travelling. We don't know their telephone number until they write."

"If you told Mummy Mellie was ill, she'd come home!" Jayne said, suddenly lifting her voice and starting to bawl.

Alison and Clare exchanged startled glances, both thinking the same thing. "Jayne, did you—?" Clare began, in a shocked voice, but Jayne interjected with an indignant voice: "Well, I ate some too

191

and I didn't get ill! She shouldn't have been such a pig!"

"Oh, those children!" Clare exploded. "Listen, Jayne, where did you get them? You must tell us!"

"No, don't shake her, Clare!" Alison said, pushing her sister away. "Come upstairs with me, honey, and we'll give you a nice wash and—"

Alison broke off, too, then, as the note of Jayne's howls changed. "She's going to be sick," Alison said, and scooping the child up in her arms, she made a dash for the bathroom. Clare went to make a cup of tea. She felt she needed one, and Alison would, too, when she came down. Alison stopped upstairs to undress Jayne and put her to bed with a hot-water bottle, and when she came downstairs again she looked very serious indeed.

"I wonder they weren't both more ill!" she said. "Do you know what she just told me? She didn't tell us untruths at first— she just left a lot out."

"Oh, very nice. What's the difference?" Clare said, bitterly, pouring boiling water on to the tea, and setting the pot to brew. "That child!"

"Yes, but the whole point is, although they got the chocolates out of Susan's drawer, it was only because they'd hidden them there in the first place. They came from next door."

"What, where the measles is? Oh, very good!"

"They were stale ones. They'd been left out in the rain all night, and Mrs. Brown said they were to be thrown away, but Billy kept them to play with and dared the girls to eat them. Well, you know Jayne— she can't resist a dare."

"It so happens she made Mellie eat them too!"

"Because she knows chocolates make Mellie sick and it would be a way of getting Susan home again—or so Jayne thought."

"Too complicated for me," Clare said, after staring incredulously at her sister. "Jayne doesn't think so deeply. She's just a selfish brat and she needs a good shaking," she said vigorously. "All your coaxing and loving methods don't do the slightest good, Alison, in the long run. She's still a brat!"

"Yes, well, now I've discovered what's

made them both ill, I must phone Raymond and let him know," Alison said, going to the telephone in what Clare considered indecent haste.

She set cups and saucers on a tray and some biscuits and took the whole load into the sitting-room to pour out. Alison was talking earnestly into the receiver.

The conversation deteriorated into a series of single affirmatives, and finally Alison put the receiver down.

"What did he say?" Clare couldn't help asking.

"He's very worried about the children. He's coming over this evening, after surgery."

Clare looked closely at her sister. "Are you worried, too? You know more about these things than I do. How serious do you think it is?"

Alison's eyes were troubled. "Mellie's colour is back and she's sleeping peacefully, but Jayne isn't so good."

"Well, do you think it's serious enough to send for Susan and Tony?" Clare said impatiently.

"Oh, Clare, so long as you can be efficient and organising, you know where you're going, don't you?" Alison said, half laughing, half ruefully. "I wish I had your sort of mind."

"Why?"

"Oh, I might have managed my own life better. About the children, no, I don't think it's serious enough to disturb Susan and Tony, so soon after they have got away for this precious holiday of theirs. No, I'm sure Raymond would have been the first to say so, if he had thought that was necessary."

Clare chafed horribly at having nothing to do. She decided to turn one of the rooms out. Susan's house-cleaning was sketchy in the extreme, and so long as she was fairly quiet, Alison agreed that it could do no harm.

She found a nylon overall of Susan's, and tied up her hair in a check duster, and settled down to a session of furniture polishing, and removing lampshades to wash them.

She and Alison had a snack meal in the kitchen and Clare went back to her work, finding an outlet for her problems and irritations in sheer hard rubbing.

Alison spent her time between the two

bedrooms. Jayne was exceedingly fretful, and Mellie inclined to be demanding now she was feeling better.

That was how Raymond Shaw found the two girls, when he knocked on the door later that evening, and getting no answer, opened the door and walked in.

Clare heard him. She leaned her face against the mirror she had been energetically cleaning, and closed her eyes. It wasn't reasonable to want so badly to rush to the door and let him in. Besides, she reminded herself, he hadn't come to see her. He could see her any day, and he never bothered to look.

She called out, "You can go upstairs—do you mind? I'm doing something I can't leave. You'll find Alison with one or other of the children."

She returned to the cleaning of the mirror. Half of it was covered in the white quick-drying liquid that the instructions assured her would, when wiped off, leave a brilliant lasting shine. There was a great area of blur, and a small patch of reasonable cleanness, in which she studied herself, without make-up, without hair showing; an aloof, cool, clever face and a pair of fine eyes, a face that wouldn't send men running to her, she told herself crossly. Least of all one man.

She saw him in the clean patch of mirror. Standing leaning against the lintel, watching her with a curious expression on his face.

She turned round on him. "I thought you were in a hurry to see the children?"

"I am. I'm going upstairs in a minute. What are you doing housework for, Clare?"

"It needs doing. I've got nothing else to do. Ewan gave me the day off to help Alison," she said shortly.

Ewan's name didn't help. It always seemed to produce an "atmosphere". Raymond Shaw said, "I see. All right, I'll go up," and with a stiff little nod he left her.

She heard their voices later. Raymond's and Alison's, talking quietly together; on and on the voices went.

Clare went and shut the door of the room so that she shouldn't hear them, but they were above her, and their voices penetrated through the ceiling.

She finished cleaning the mirror and put

the dusters and cleaning materials away. Her back and arms were aching. She was tired, desperately tired. She would have given the world for a hot bath, but she supposed she had better save the water in case Alison needed it. Besides, the bathroom was too near where the children were. It would disturb them.

Then a walk was the next best thing, Clare decided. She took a hasty wash, and combed her hair, ready to go out when she knew the verdict on the children.

Raymond and Alison came downstairs together, and Alison walked him to the front gate. Talking all the time. They stood there, Alison looking up at him while he talked. When he finally took his leave of her, he laid a hand on her arm for a moment, and whatever he was saying, it brought a huge smile to both their faces. Alison waved to him as he got in his car and drove away.

"Well, what was all that about?" Clare asked her sister, when she came back.

"He's so *nice*," Alison said warmly. "The children are going to be *all right*."

"Good! Then we won't need to expect him here in the evening any more, will we?" Clare said, feeling cross and unreasonable, and not liking herself very much for it.

"Yes, we will," Alison said, in a surprised voice. "This has been such a scare to us that he's going to drop in every evening for the rest of the time Susan's away, just to make sure everything's all right."

10

THERE was a lot of work for Clare to pull up when she returned to Ewan Burnett. There were proofs in to be read and corrected, too, and much more research work to be done. She was glad, because it gave Ewan far less time to discuss their personal association. Nevertheless, it came up, inevitably.

She braced herself for it, after they had made inroads into the backlog of work.

"Are you free, now, Clare, from domestic ties?" he asked her, as she was putting the cover on her typewriter some days later. "Really free, so that we can make plans of our own?"

She had to admit she was. Life at home was settling into a steady pattern, with the evenings taken up with Raymond Shaw's visit. Alison prepared for his visit with as much care as if it had been Keith Everton. She fussed over her appearance, had something nice for a snack supper, all ready and a table nicely laid by the fire. The children would be looking nice, too, for the doctor's cursory glance at them, before he came downstairs to talk to Alison.

"Oh, yes, we're quite free," Clare was driven to say.

"Good! Then what about tonight—or is the notice too short?"

"No, I can manage tonight," Clare said, wondering what her sister would have to say about it. Alison had a strong sense of the proprieties, due, Clare supposed, to her hospital training. She looked forward to Raymond Shaw's little chats with her, while Clare was busy in some other room. She would be disappointed to find Clare going out.

"Then I thought we would do a show tonight, and some dinner."

"Will Mrs. Hewitt be there, too?" Clare asked idly.

Ewan was affronted at that. "It isn't a joke, Clare!"

"I didn't mean it as a joke, believe me! But what is the purpose of our being out together if she isn't to see us?"

"Someone will see us, be very sure of that, and see that she knows about it. You may not realise it, Clare, but she's been on the telephone twice to me in your absence, to try and find out as much as she can about it."

Alison took the news very quietly. "I did rather expect it, Clare dear, if, as you say, you might be engaged to him soon. Don't worry. I don't mind a bit."

But if Alison didn't mind, Raymond Shaw did. Next morning he asked abruptly, "Where did you get to, last night?"

"I went to a show and dinner," she said.

He didn't go so far as to ask who with, but he stared at her so long, with a waiting air, that she found herself adding, "I went with Ewan Burnett."

"I see."

He didn't repeat the experiment of taking her with him on his rounds, and she was glad. She hadn't enjoyed being with him in the car, knowing that all the time he was thinking about Alison.

"Have you heard from the children's parents yet?" he asked a little later.

"No. I expected a card or something, but perhaps they're moving around too much. Or maybe they're thinking it might unsettle the children."

"Do you really think that's likely?" he asked with a faint smile and a lift of one eyebrow.

"No, I don't, to be honest, but Alison does, and she seems to understand them better than I do."

For a short while that reduced them almost to the level of fellow conspirators, until he started talking about Alison, and how she was coping with the children. Inevitably the conversation drifted towards what Alison meant to do, after her month's holiday was ended.

It was time to open the surgery then, without the point having been resolved, but his mentioning Alison had unwittingly destroyed that brief contact.

It was another heavy surgery that day, and at the end of it, he said, carelessly, "I have to go over to Monks Haybury this afternoon. I suppose you wouldn't like to come?"

"But I have to go up to Wycherley Holt," she said, in surprise.

"You got the afternoon off, for apparently no better reason than to do some of your cousin's house-cleaning," he said unreasonably.

"That wasn't the reason. Alison said you didn't think I'd be able to get time off to help her when the children were ill."

"So you wangled time off to prove how wrong I was about Burnett—is that it?"

"No, of course it isn't! I'm only saying that that was the real reason why I got time off—"

"Burnett being, of course, the salt of the earth, and deeply touched by the illness of children?"

"—and now I've got to work extra hard to make up for lost time," she finished, deliberately ignoring his thrust.

Relations were now strained between them and she was glad that she had agreed to go out with Ewan again that night.

Life was settling into a pattern. Clare was made unhappily aware, by the District Nurse the next day, that she wasn't the only one to notice the doctor's interest in the children's welfare.

"Why, Clare, dear! I was hoping I would run into you! You can give me the inside story and explode these wild rumours once and for all! Who is the doctor keen on—you or Alison? And if it's you, then what are you doing getting your name linked with Mr. Burnett? Everyone's saying they're seeing you with him in all the best places!"

"I shouldn't listen to a thing, if I were you, Miss Quinney. He's very kind to me, and I go out working with him."

"What, dining at The Three Drovers, and dancing afterwards? If that's how you young things earn your living nowadays, then I wish I was young again!" and she laughed.

Clare wondered why she hadn't said what Ewan had wanted her to say: that she was about to become engaged to him. Ewan didn't know the term "going steady" and somehow it didn't seem to fit an association with him.

What's the matter with you, she asked herself fiercely. Do you think anything's going to change, just because you're holding back from saying what it's your job to say? Do you think Raymond Shaw will ever see you as a person, you idiot, least of all fall in love with you?

So she added, "In confidence, I might —I just might be thinking seriously about Ewan Burnett."

And that wasn't really burning her boats, she assured herself.

She wasn't quite so sure of that when she reached home that afternoon.

Alison had got both the children downstairs that afternoon, and now they were washed and ready for bed, in their fluffy dressing-gowns by the fire, having stories read to them. No bedtime stories for these two: they liked tales of animals who dressed and talked like sophisticated humans and carried out crimes that would raise the hair on the heads of human police.

". . . and he swore a dreadful oath and shot PC. Dog dead, and putting a dark handkerchief over his snout, he rushed into the bank and shouted 'This is a hold-up', and all the animals dived for cover . . ." Alison read, with as much gusto as if she were really enjoying the story.

"Disgusting!" Clare murmured, rumpling Mellie's shock of curls with an affectionate hand. "At your age, Melissandra Masters!"

"He kills six policemen dead before the

end of the book—I know, I looked!" Jayne said, scowling.

"Surely the doctor won't come tonight to look at these two?" Clare exploded. "They couldn't be in better health! Look at them!"

"He is. He likes to make sure," Alison said, and Clare fancied her face was rather pink.

She came into Clare's bedroom after she had settled the children down for the night, and she stood regarding her sister.

"Where are you going *tonight?*"

"Film." Clare turned this way and that, surveying her new jersey suit. "Does it look all right? Is it *me?*"

"Yes, it's very nice," Alison said doubtfully.

"It isn't really, is it? I'm being too adventurous with new clothes—that's what you mean, isn't it?"

"No, Clare, dear. It's just—well, Mr. Burnett is rich. Don't you think you ought to buy something more—I mean, this is very nice for ordinary occasions."

"No. I'm not going to blue every penny I've got, just because he has a big big balance. He must take me as I am," Clare said, nettled. Alison was right, of course. She ought to have bought a more expensive outfit, but she had happened to like this one.

"Aren't you in love with him, Clare?" Alison asked, in a troubled voice.

"Do I look as if I'm in love?" Clare asked, rather curiously. "I wouldn't have thought so."

"Yes, you do, sometimes, but not quite in the way I meant. You see, the first I heard of it was when the children said you were in love with your boss and he never really saw you, I could believe that."

Clare looked startled.

"Clare, dear, don't think I'm prying," Alison said earnestly. "You and I have always been close, and I did tell you about —my troubles."

"Did you?" Clare said shortly. "I don't think you did!"

"As much as I could," Alison said, with difficulty. "The point is, you've changed. Only recently."

"How have I changed?"

"It's hard to say. As if you were still sort of unhappy over being in love, but as if you no longer care, too. And that doesn't make sense, because whereas at one time Mr. Burnett just saw you as an employee, now he is wanting to be engaged to you, isn't he? And you're still not happy."

In sheer defence, because it wouldn't be long before Alison guessed the truth at this rate, Clare said shortly, "Perhaps I want to be loved, not just married!"

"Oh, Clare, I'm sorry!" Alison was at once contrite, believing she had put her finger on the true trouble and been clumsy about it. "I didn't mean . . ."

"Forget it, darling!"

"I suppose that explains why you're so scratchy with everyone else. But you don't have to be like that with Raymond as well, do you?"

"Now why shouldn't I? What's so special about him? I'm scratchy when other people irritate me, so why not him too? And believe me, he irritates me very much at times!"

"I do so wish you could be nice to him, Clare."

"Why? Isn't it enough that you are nice to him, honey?"

"But you do like him, don't you?" Alison persisted.

Clare faced her sister, laughing in sheer exasperation. "What's the matter? Is it that you can see no wrong in him so I have to be goo-ey over him too?"

"I'm not goo-ey over him!" Alison said indignantly.

"Then just what are you, I should like to know?"

Alison flushed poppy-red. "I just think he's the nicest person I know!"

"And that of course is all the difference in the world!" Clare teased.

It struck her as the oddest thing in the world that she could manage to joke and lie about Raymond and her feelings for him. Her best Pagliacci act, she derided herself. Make fun of your breaking heart, girl, that's the stuff!

"I think so," Alison said, in answer to her remark.

"Ally," she said, suddenly serious, "I don't mind what you do, no matter what it is, so long as you're happy. Do you understand what I mean? Well, are you going to be happy, like this?"

"I don't know what you mean," Alison said painfully.

"Well, Keith Everton. Is it really all over, forgotten, dead? Because if it isn't, don't let yourself be caught on the rebound. That way isn't for you, my dear."

Alison looked outraged, and pulled away from Clare's grasp. "I told you, I don't want to mention him, ever again!" and she ran out of the room.

Mellie suddenly called out, and Alison went in to her. Clare, furious with herself, rummaged in her drawer for stockings.

Then she remembered she had lent her latest pair to Alison. Oh, well, if they hadn't been used yet, she'd just have to get them back again, she supposed.

Alison was using Susan's small chest of drawers as a bedside table. The top drawer usually stood open a few inches. It was too difficult to shut, as a rule. Clare leaned down and looked in it, but the new packet of nylons wasn't there. There was, however, a letter lying open, hastily stuffed in there. It was in Keith's handwriting. Clare recognised it—he had written to Susan once, about his coming engagement to Alison. It was unmistakable writing; thick, black, squarish. Now Clare came to look closer, there were several envelopes in there, and bits of Keith's thick black scrawl could be seen on all of them.

Poor Alison, she must have brought all his old letters with her and been reading them, perhaps while Clare was out in the evening. Perhaps that was why she had been crying that night, the night Keith was supposed to have telephoned.

Clare got to her feet. How could she have been so clumsy as to mention him just now? But if Alison was still grieving for Keith, why was she getting interested in the doctor? Rebound, as she herself had just suggested?

Clare knew that she was no use with other people's love affairs. Her mind was best with a problem needing cool calculation, efficiency. She could look clearly at her own problem, and work it out, but to attempt to assess what was best for Alison was beyond her. Raymond Shaw would make Alison a wonderful husband; kind, warm and affectionate, and if he was hot-tempered at times, and bearish, Alison would be able to handle that. But was it the best thing for the doctor to have a wife who secretly still yearned for her old love?

"Is it really any business of mine?" Clare asked herself fiercely, as the imperious toot of Ewan's car horn sounded outside. "Raymond Shaw wouldn't thank me for interfering, I'm certain!"

Yet she couldn't rid herself of what seemed like a tragic future for both of them, all that evening. Ewan leaned forward once or twice and peered into her face.

"What's the matter, Clare? Don't you care for the film? Shall we go somewhere else?"

"No, I'm loving it!" she lied. It was awful, the number of times she evaded the truth nowadays, she thought, in despair.

Yet there was a limit to the amount of pretending she could do, and in the end she pleaded a headache and cut short the evening.

In the car at the end of the road—as far as Clare would allow Ewan to bring her that night on the grounds that it might wake the children—he tried to kiss her.

"Now why should you mind, Clare?" he

asked her, in very real surprise. "We are trying to do this thing convincingly and the best way is to form habits. If we act as an engaged couple would—"

"We're not engaged yet!" she couldn't resist reminding him.

"Then let's be."

"No. No, not yet," she pleaded.

"But why not? I've warned you about it, heaven knows."

"But it wasn't in the original plan, was it, Ewan? Oh, I know I said I would, if it was necessary, but give me a little more time. I'm used to thinking of you as one of my bosses, and it's so hard to get used to all this. Please, Ewan."

Oddly that seemed to please him. "All right, my dear. A good many young women would be only too anxious to fall into a fellow's arms. Perhaps I'm old-fashioned, but frankly that type of young woman terrifies me."

"Then, shall we say goodnight now? I'm really very tired."

He held her arms. "I think you should learn to get used to a starter kiss, don't you think?" he said, whimsically, and he leaned forward and kissed her gently on the mouth.

After a startled pause, she said a hasty goodnight, scrambled out of the car and fled.

I didn't like it, she told herself all the way up the street. What am I going to do? He'll hold me to an engagement and I won't be able to get out of it, and keep my job at the same time—I know I won't. And if I go through with it I shall hate every minute of my life from then on. What am I going to do?

The lights of Susan's house were on: brightly downstairs, dimly upstairs. That meant only the landing light, shining through the open doors of the children's rooms. A woman's figure moved about. That would be Alison upstairs, quietly putting things away in the drawers.

Clare suddenly decided to tell Alison all about this strange job she was doing extra for Ewan. Quite suddenly she wanted to confide in someone, and the thought of Alison, sweet comfortable domestic cosy Alison, made her want to unload her troubles at once.

She let herself in softly and stood with

her back to the door, quietly letting the latch slip into place. Alison wouldn't thank her for waking Mellie at this time of the evening.

The chiming clock in the sitting-room softly pranged out nine hours. It was warm and inviting inside, after the sharp cold night air. Clare drew a deep breath and prepared to go upstairs and take her things off, and tell her sister she wanted to talk to her.

She wasn't prepared to hear Alison's voice come from the sitting-room, near at hand. "You don't understand. You just don't understand!"

A man's voice answered. A soft murmur, to which Alison again protested. Who was in there with Alison—Keith Everton? He leapt at once into her mind. And who, for goodness sake, was upstairs —one of the neighbours, Clare supposed. Alison and her strong sense of the proprieties!

And then the man raised his voice slightly, so that Clare recognised it.

"Alison, my dear, sweet soul, that's no way to talk. You can't spend your life running away from love, just because it's

216

hurt you once. Look at me," and to the listening Clare, with a shock, came the realisation that it was Raymond Shaw in there talking to Alison.

11

IT was such a shock that Clare didn't know what to do at first, and then it was too late to do anything, for whoever was upstairs started to come down.

It was Mrs. Brown from next door. "Oh, there you are!" she said to Clare. "You're back early! Oh well, that's nice, because I can toddle off home and see my television show after all."

Alison and the doctor came out then, but they didn't seem embarrassed to see Clare.

Raymond smiled in a pleased way. "Oh, I'm glad Clare's back early. Now, Alison, take my advice, go and relax, and stop worrying about anything!"

The hand he put on Alison's shoulder was as informal and casual as he would accord the young daughter of any patient, and Mrs. Brown seemed in no way disturbed.

Clare automatically moved aside for

Alison to walk down to the gate with him, but she didn't tonight. She looked as if she might be near tears, too.

Mrs. Brown told Alison not to hesitate to call her in on any other occasion, and bustled away. The sisters were left alone, and Alison appeared uncertain for the first time.

"You're back very early," she said at last.

"I'm sorry if it's messed things up for you," Clare offered. "If you'd said Mrs. Brown could come—"

"Yes, what then?"

"I was only going to say I made the excuse to come home in case you wanted a break. You have the children every night, and anyway, I was fed up with the film. I said I was tired, and pretty soon I'd have had a headache."

"But I thought you were in love with him and couldn't get out with him enough!" Alison exclaimed. "Is anything wrong, Clare? You haven't quarrelled with him, have you?"

"No, of course not." Clare moved down the hall and took her gloves off. "You couldn't quarrel with Ewan," she said, and stripping off her jacket, she went into the sitting-room and spread her hands to the blaze.

"I think I'll make a pot of tea," Alison said mechanically.

"Are the children all right?"

"Yes. Yes, they're fine! I've told Raymond over and over again that he needn't come any more in the evenings. He must be tired out, but he insists on coming."

Clare followed Alison out to the kitchen. "I might say the same to you as you said just now to me—I thought you liked him being here with you."

"Well, I do!" Alison shifted restlessly. "I like talking to him. He's easy to talk to."

"He sounded very fond of you, when I came in." It wasn't in Clare not to let Alison know she had heard something.

But Alison didn't seem at all embarrassed. "What did you hear him saying?" she asked with interest in her voice.

"I hope you don't mind—I came in and I just couldn't help hearing—he seemed to be giving you advice about love and life, that sort of thing. He sounded very fond of you."

"Oh, yes, he is. He was giving me advice, too. I told him before, he loves giving advice. He gave me some advice about you, too."

"He *what?*"

"He's very fond of you, too, Clare," Alison said seriously. "Somehow the conversation always seems to get round to you. I've noticed it before, so tonight I told him how anxious I've been about you and Mr. Burnett."

"Now look here, Alison, I don't want you to talk to the doctor about Ewan and me!" Clare said angrily.

"You don't like it? Funny, he didn't seem to like it, either. But you see, he knows something to Mr. Burnett's discredit. I hate saying this to you, but I feel I have to."

"Then don't. He doesn't know anything. He's just prejudiced against my other employer—he always has been—and he listens to gossip about Ewan."

Alison said nothing to that, and went on making the tea.

"How was it Mrs. Brown was here?" Clare asked again.

"Oh, that! She came to borrow some more sugar. I'm getting rather tired of it. I think she was only inquisitive. So I said she'd better stay for a bit, in case the telephone rang while the doctor was looking at the children, and when we came downstairs I asked her to put the airing away and stay with me for a while. She agreed I ought to have a chaperone," Alison finished with a puckish smile. "It was a good thing Raymond didn't hear that—he'd have gone off the handle. He doesn't like her."

"Neither do I," Clare snorted.

But Mrs. Brown had unwittingly staved off another of those stiff "atmospheres" that seemed to interpose themselves between the sisters lately, and they sat amicably discussing clothes and the children until it was bedtime.

It was that evening that the first of the postcards appeared from Susan and Tony, delivered at the wrong house while the occupiers had been away. After that, a shoal of postcards arrived, and from them Clare and Alison learned that the children's parents weren't keeping to their original schedule. "Have had a chance of going to La Fidelle Des Roses," Susan wrote ecstatically, "with some people staying here. Will let you know the address later."

So for the moment Clare and Alison had no way of contacting them, but as the children were practically well again, it hardly seemed to matter.

It was the following evening that Mrs. Brown came to borrow some tea.

"You'd better buy a quarter from us, then you'll be in the clear," Clare suggested. Like Alison, she didn't like all this lending. Mrs. Brown had the trick of sailing off with a cupful of this and half a cupful of that, and so far she had paid nothing back, and Susan would be furious.

"Don't be silly, dear," Mrs. Brown said, "if I had any cash left, I'd trot down to the shop on the corner, but I haven't till the week-end. It's all right, your cousin always obliges me like this."

Clare knew that wasn't true, but Alison didn't, and she wavered.

Mrs. Brown said chattily, "Oh, by the way, I hope you won't mind me saying this, but I think you ought to know. There's a rumour going round about your Mr. Burnett, Clare."

Clare said, "Here's a packet of tea. Take the whole quarter, and I've made a note of it. I'm afraid I'll have to ask you for the same brand back, because my cousin doesn't like any other."

"I don't suppose she'll bother me to pay it back," Mrs. Brown said comfortably. "But about your Mr. Burnett, they're saying he had his driving licence suspended for ever such a long time, on account of a nasty accident, and it was supposed to be his fault that the man died only they weren't sure."

She paused and waited, but Clare had drifted off, leaving Alison to cope; but hearing Ewan's name, Clare came back.

"I can tell you that that rumour is quite untrue," she said coldly. "Did you want anything else, Mrs. Brown?"

Mrs. Brown looked taken aback, then she decided to turn huffy, and went off down the path with her quarter packet of tea.

"Oh, dear, I wish you hadn't been like that to her, Clare! She's such a scandalmonger, she'll put that story all over the place with embellishments! I could have handled it tactfully, if you'd let me." She looked put out. "Besides, she—"

"Besides, she won't come in and chaperone you and Raymond again?" Clare couldn't help finishing. "Sorry, I suppose I shouldn't have said that, but really!"

"I wasn't going to say that, Clare," Alison said evenly.

"That's good. Because you won't have to bother tonight. I shall be at home. Oh, I'll keep out of your way if you want to talk to him, but I can't have that woman saying things like that about Ewan."

"Even if it were true?" Alison said softly.

"It isn't true! Is it?" Clare asked, suddenly suspicious. "Have you any reason to think it is?"

"Raymond said something of the sort himself."

Clare turned to the window, and stood drumming on the sill. "Well, if it were true, what about it? Lots of people must have the same thing happen to them. Goodness, you don't have to make an outcast of a man because he has had a bit of bad luck on the roads."

"There was something else, Clare, that Raymond told me," Alison persevered.

"Well, I don't want to hear it. If you two like to sit in a huddle discussing other people—"

"He doesn't do that sort of thing! He was worried about you because people are talking about you being seen about with him and that Miss Quinney is saying you're going to be engaged to him."

"I'm sick of this gossiping place!" Clare said, going to to the door. "I don't want to hear anything else about him!"

"But I have to tell you, Clare. There was some sort of scandal about a girl."

Clare began to laugh. "Now I know it's all a lot of gossip. It's funny, it really is! To think that a rumour of that sort could start about Ewan of all people! He's so shy of designing women that he—"

She shut her mouth suddenly. She had been going to confide in Alison last night about it, but the desire to tell her had passed, because she believed in her heart that even if Alison weren't as fond of the doctor as he was of her, she was in the habit of telling him everything and Clare didn't want Raymond to know about this odd arrangement she had slipped into with Ewan. Raymond would condemn Ewan's scheme out of hand. She knew that without having to be told.

"Go on," Alison prompted gently.

"Forget it. It's an awful rumour, and if I were you, I wouldn't encourage such things!"

They weren't so easy to forget, however. As Clare went through her drawers and found some nylons to wash, and a few things needing mending, she remembered the odd remarks Ewan had made, in the early days when she had worked for him; remarks that had meant little then but which clicked into place now. There was the day when he had come back from driving his new car and had seemed boyishly pleased. He had been full of it and had remarked that it was wonderful to be driving again.

Driving again . . . She had thought at the time that he was referring to the departure of his chauffeur, leaving him to drive the car himself. But come to think of it, why had he had a chauffeur in the first place, if he had enjoyed driving so much himself? Did it really mean that his suspended licence had then been renewed? If so, that meant that that rumour was true.

Then if that rumour was true, might not the other rumour be true? It had been a phoney sort of reason that he had given for this curious pretend engagement of theirs (which, if she wasn't careful, would be formally announced at any moment), and one which had struck her as out of line. Ewan seemed to be quite confident with her, and indeed only seemed to be afraid of girls when he remembered to be, or when the formidable Mrs. Lattimore Hewitt was around.

That woman had been on the telephone every day since that first evening Clare had been out with Ewan, but every day she had carried out her instructions and said that Mr. Burnett couldn't be disturbed. Sooner or later he would have to talk to her. Did she know something about his past? Was that why he was afraid of her?

Now all Clare's old apprehensions about him rushed back. Angrily she told herself she was being swayed by the rumours, just as she had scathingly said other people were being swayed.

Look at it from the other angle, she told herself. Who didn't like Ewan? People who wanted to know him socially because he was the only successful writer in the district, and naturally they resented his exclusive attitude. Who did like Ewan? The police, because of his generosity to their charities—and that went for anyone else locally who asked him for money; he never refused them. The same went for his personal staff, ruling out the chauffeur. Clare wasn't sure why he had left exactly, but he hadn't left with kindly feelings towards Ewan.

Anyone else? Why, yes, his writing friends—scores of them, successful people like himself, who came from London. Sophisticated people. (People, her senses whispered, who wouldn't be unduly put out if they found out he had had such things as a suspended driving licence or one scandal in his life.)

Her arguments didn't satisfy her and she decided to ask him next day if he had heard about these rumours and what she could do to quash them.

It comforted her, that thought. But before she could do any such thing, she had Raymond Shaw to face.

"I didn't ask you last night, Clare, in front of that awful Mrs. Brown, but what made you come home so early—it was barely nine o'clock. Did you have any trouble while you were out with Burnett?"

"Trouble? What do you mean?"

"Now don't go all prickly with me, Clare. You know very well what I mean. You looked rather shaken. I thought at first that perhaps you might have seen an accident on the roads. After all, it doesn't follow that one has been involved in one, to get thoroughly shaken. You know yourself that some of the people we've had in here have been mere bystanders, knocked over by what they've seen!"

"Oh." She was relieved. "No, I didn't see an accident, Raymond, and it's good of you to be so concerned about me, but I assure you, it was nothing more than a headache threatening."

He seemed far from satisfied. "Where did you go? Well, somewhere where there was a lot of fug? Cigarette smoke in an enclosed atmosphere is the worst possible thing at the end of a hard day such as you have!"

"We went to see a film," she said shortly. Her days might not be so hard if he didn't constantly clash with her, she told herself, outraged at his misplaced solicitude.

"A film! The important Mr. Burnett can settle for nothing better than a film! The times I've thought of asking you to go to the flicks with me, and each time I've abandoned the idea on the grounds that it would take something far more exciting than that to tempt you."

She was wide-eyed with surprise. "You? You had ideas of taking me to the pictures? Now really, you may know my cousin well, but you don't have to feel so responsible for Alison and me!"

"Who said I felt responsible?"

"Well, going round every night to the house."

"Don't you like me doing that, Clare?"

"It's nothing to do with me. It's for Alison to say whether she likes that part of it or not. I'm not usually in. Now you say you've thought of taking me to the pictures! Why? To protect me from the clutches of the Ewan Burnetts of this world? I'm quite able to take care of myself, I assure you!"

"Well, I'm not so certain of that," he said, after a marked pause. "The District Nurse tells me you didn't deny being about to be engaged to marry Burnett. That isn't really true, is it, Clare? I've been rather amused at your excursions with him lately, but I didn't really think you'd let it go as far as that!"

"You keep on about him so! Why? What have you got against him?"

"Plenty. He's not your type, Clare."

"Really! And what *is* my type, may I ask?"

Old Dr. Shaw threw the door open, and stood there. "If I'm to start surgery this morning, might I have a bit of peace and quiet, you two? Or don't you mind half the district sitting with their ears flapping, listening to your lover's quarrel?"

Clare was speechless with fury. Raymond went red, and turned away to get his bag.

"Yes, you'd better do something useful," the older man growled. "Go up to the farm. They've been telephoning again.

And take her with you—you can finish your row on the way."

"Dr. Shaw, I've got my work to do here," Clare said, as he made to shut the door on them and return to the surgery.

The older man looked at her with the suspicion of a twinkle in his eyes. "My dear, I am not yet too senile to put out my hand and pick up the telephone in the surgery, and I'm quite capable of filling in a few cards in the file index. It's *his* idea to keep you here as secretary, not mine!"

He shut the door on them then with determination.

Clare turned on Raymond. "Is this true? Don't you really need me here?"

He shrugged. "That's a silly question. You seem to find plenty to do to help me during your mornings. You should know whether your efforts are necessary or not."

"Your father always manages without me. He seems to prefer it. Why don't you?"

He looked steadily at her for a minute, then he returned to his bag. "Because I'm the sort of chap who likes a bit of help, I suppose. We can't all be alike."

She stood irresolute. "But you said you

could use me in the afternoons as well, if I weren't working up at Wycherley Holt. Wasn't that true?"

He didn't answer that one.

"No, it wasn't true," she said bitterly. "You don't like Ewan Burnett and you didn't want me to work for him so you made it up about needing me here. I think that was rotten of you!"

"You heard what my father said about everyone listening out there," he reminded her mildly.

"Oh, there are times—!" she fumed. "Well, now I know how it is, I'm not staying here. I'll go and work for Ewan in the mornings as well. He wants me to."

She ripped off her white coat.

"You're working here at the moment," he reminded her.

"Your father has told me to clear out with you to the farm. If I'm no more use than that, then I'm not staying!"

She stormed out of the house, but by the time she was at the bottom of the road she was sorry she had been so hasty. He could now accuse her of being childish and bad-tempered and he would be right. But it had hurt so much to find that she hadn't really been needed there all that urgently. Useful, perhaps, sometimes, but not *needed*, not every day, every minute, as she had wanted to be needed by Raymond. And his father had been quietly watching, gently amused.

She liked old Dr. Shaw very much, but she was so cross with him at this moment that she couldn't think straight.

Well, now was her opportunity to go up to Wycherley Holt and tell Ewan she was free to work for him in the mornings as well, but somehow the inclination had gone.

She wandered up and down the High Street, looking unseeingly in the shop windows. She couldn't rid herself of the way Raymond had looked at her. Rather like the way he had looked at her that day at Padcross lake, when they had been quarrelling. She couldn't see for the mist in front of her eyes, and then she cleared it by blinking hard, she found she was looking in the mirror at the back of the local hairdresser's window.

That sudden unexpected personal view in a mirror is always shattering. She saw herself as rather young and not very sure of herself, her hair windblown, her dark eyes still nursing the hurt and the yearning for Raymond Shaw. That yearning that would never be appeased, not if she married Ewan Burnett and went to the end of the world!

She decided to go in and get her hair done. It was as good a way as any to spend a bad morning she had stolen from an employer, she supposed.

There was, by sheer good luck, someone free at that moment. Clare took her coat off and went in.

The girl was new, and didn't launch herself into conversation with Clare as her usual hairdresser did. Clare was free to relax but soon to unwillingly listen to the conversation from the cubicle on the other side of her.

Vaguely she recognised the voice; brittle, high-pitched, filled with laughter, yet not a young voice. Inevitably it began to descend to personalities and to talk about Ewan.

"I wish I knew where I had *seen* that girl before. Somewhere locally. I don't believe that he is really about to be engaged to her, yet you should have seen the way he looked at her. Perhaps it isn't an *engagement* he's about to propose, but *something else*."

"Oh, Mrs. Lattimore Hewitt, you are naughty!" The hairdresser was evidently playing safe, the discomfited Clare thought. Never upset the customer, especially if there is a big tip coming.

Her own girl pretended she couldn't hear, but Clare writhed just the same.

"It was almost indecent, the way they looked at each other, and my poor little Francine was almost in *tears*. As I said to her when we reached home, she doesn't know what she's been *saved* from."

"Was she a friend of Mr. Burnett's then, madam?"

"We've been friends with him for some *time* and it was always *understood* that if he married, it would be my Francine. He was so *fond* of her! And then to invite that *girl*, that night of *all* nights!"

"Was it a special night, then, madam?"

"Of *course* it was! We had invited him to join *our* party. Two days before, that was. And he said he didn't think he could manage it but he would *try*. Then he said he thought he would have to bring someone along and I said, but of course —bring who you like. Then he said he couldn't. And then there he was, sitting there, with this girl, just as if nothing previously had been *said* about the evening. You see, it was my *birthday*."

The hairdresser made appropriate noises. Clare remembered her. Dawn, they called her. A girl who loved gossip. It would be all over the town by lunchtime. Never before had Clare realised how much gossip flew back and forth in Rexmundham.

Her own girl put the drier on, but even the high-pitched moan of it couldn't quite obliterate that highly inflammable conversation in the next cubicle.

From it Clare learned that Ewan had previously lived in London, and that he had a holiday place in the South of France; a place he had promised to loan Mrs. Hewitt. She bandied names with a complete indifference of how her voice carried; names of writing friends of Ewan's whom Clare knew, names of friends of her own. She sacrificed kindness for wit, if she could find something to say about any of them which would make the hairdresser laugh. She even poked gentle fun at her own daughter who, she said, needed the teeniest "push" from Mamma to get her settled in life.

What a horrible woman, Clare thought, with a shudder. She now faced the problem of whether she should let Ewan know about this or not. He might resent her talking about his friends, but if it got around by other means, he might feel that Clare ought to have told him about it. But at least Mrs. Lattimore Hewitt didn't seem to know about the rumours that were circulating about Ewan's driving accident or that other girl—*if* they were true.

If . . . Clare sat with her eyes closed and asked herself if it would really matter very much if it were true. She tried to picture herself married to Ewan. Would she mind very much if that had happened in her husband's life? The answer was very swift. If she loved him, then it was no. Quite unreasonably it would be yes, if she didn't love him. And she didn't love Ewan.

By the time the drier came off her head, and her ears hadn't yet adjusted themselves to being without that high-pitched whine, Mrs. Hewitt's drier was off too.

But Mrs. Hewitt was having other things done, and she had settled down to the whole morning.

With a start Clare realised she was still talking about Ewan, and she certainly did seem to know about that accident, but the bias was now in Ewan's favour. Somewhere between Clare's drier being started and stopped, Mrs. Hewitt had changed her attack. She was no longer anti-Ewan.

"Clearly it was the other man's fault. Mr. Burnett was a marvellous driver, and so careful on the roads, and he never ever had a drink before driving. Of course, that girl lied. I could see that, when I read over the accounts in the newspapers."

"The London papers, madam?"

"No, silly girl, you haven't been listening. The Monks Haybury Gazette carried a very big splash because it was a local accident. Just eighteen months ago. He was down there to look for a place. He wanted to live in Monks Haybury, but settled for this place finally. We're far enough away not to see the Gazette here—thanks to our little Argus. The poor man doesn't want to be constantly reminded of that unhappy incident. But of course, when I heard that that girl had been *after* him, and that he broke it off with her when he saw how warm the running was getting, well . . . I just put two and two together. He's the nicest man, and not one to be caught in the toils of some designing creature, if *I* can help it!"

Mrs. Hewitt's head must have been plunged into the water then, for there were only sounds of gasps and hissing of the jet, splashings and the metallic clink of some container being crashed down.

The little girl setting Clare's hair kept her eyes down commendably, but Clare could sense she was listening avidly.

She hoped she would be able to get out of the place before Mrs. Hewitt started up again, but she wasn't so lucky.

"So whenever you hear that stupid rumour about Mr. Burnett, dear, you deny it, vigorously! You may take it from me that not a word of it was true. You know what they say—hell hath no fury like a woman scorned!"

"Yes, madam," the girl said, towelling vigorously. Clare could see the movements of the big orange towel through the chink in the curtains.

"And I don't mean to rest until I find out who this other girl is!" Mrs. Hewitt went on. "I am sure she is an adventuress who has heard how rich he is and is after his money. I just wish I could remember her name!"

Clare, sickened, hurried out of the hairdressers, and towards home.

It was too soon for lunch, so she decided to slip in and briefly explain to Alison that she had taken the morning off from the surgery, and that she was going over to Monks Haybury and would get a meal there.

Now it was imperative to go to the offices of the Monks Haybury Gazette to look up the details of that old accident. She must see the impersonal details of a newspaper report, before she could make up her own mind.

The house was empty. She searched everywhere, but neither Alison nor the children were there.

She went out into the crisp sunny air again and stood thinking. Where could they be? She was about to go and knock at a neighbour's house when a taxi drew up and a young man got out, paid the driver, and stood staring up at the house as if to make certain it was the one he wanted. And then he noticed Clare, standing in the shadow of the front hedge.

"Why, it's—it *is* Alison's sister, isn't it?" he said.

"Yes, I'm Clare. It's Keith Everton, isn't it?" she said faintly.

12

IT was some time since Clare had seen Keith Everton, and he had changed a lot. He now wore glasses, which made him look older, far more serious. His light brown hair was slicked back. Clare missed the unruly lock that had always flopped over his forehead, giving him a gay boyish air. She hadn't remembered that he was quite so tall. He was thinner. She did remember, however, that sensitive smile, and the eager friendliness in his eyes.

"I'm very glad to see you again," she said, putting out her hand. "I'm sure my sister Alison will be, too!"

He looked uncertain. "I'm not so sure about that, myself," he said at once. "We had a corking row and although I've written many times, I can't get her to make it up, so there was nothing for it but to come down here and have it out with her and see if I can persuade her not to be so silly."

"Was she silly? Look, why don't we go

indoors and talk it over? She isn't at home at the moment. I was going to ask one of the neighbours if they knew where she was. Actually I shouldn't really be at home yet—I wasn't at work this morning, and I just dropped in to tell Alison I was going to Monks Haybury."

"Monks Haybury!" he echoed. "That's a town I have always wanted to see. It's historical, isn't it?"

"It may be, but all I'm interested in is its newspaper offices. I have to look up some back numbers," Clare smiled, searching for her key again.

"Look, don't think me rude, but I've only got a couple of hours before I have to go back to London, and I would rather like to spend them with Alison. If you could find out where she is, perhaps I could go and meet her? It's less personal, somehow, to talk in the open than in the house. If she'd been at home, I was going to ask her to come walking with me to discuss it."

Clare was sympathetic. "Yes, I quite see what you mean. Now, who would know? Oh, here comes Mrs. Brown. She knows everything and everybody."

He nodded. He had keyed himself up for this meeting with Alison, and it was disconcerting to find that no one knew where Alison was or when she was likely to be back at the house.

Mrs. Brown bore down on them. "Oh, there you are, Clare! I heard someone moving about in the house and I said to myself, who would that be, because d'you see, I'd seen Alison going into his car, and I thought to myself, you won't be back yet awhile, my girl! Is it going to be an engagement soon, Clare?"

"Mrs. Brown!" Clare said, quickly, but not quickly enough to stem the tide of her garrulous neighbour's remarks. "Do you know where my sister has gone, and when she'll be back? I expect the doctor gave her a lift. Did she say?"

Mrs. Brown looked amused. "Oh, go on, do! The doctor giving her a lift, my eye! He's been in and out of this house since she arrived, on any old excuse. Anyone can see he's not really needing his little black bag when he comes to this house! Who's this, then?" she said, looking with interest at Keith's embarrassed face. "A new boy-friend of yours,

246

dear? I thought you were practically fixed up with that Mr. Burnett!"

"This is a friend of Alison's, Mrs. Brown," Clare said frigidly. "I'm afraid Mrs. Brown sees a romance blossoming if people just look at each other," she said to Keith.

He wasn't inclined to accept that. "Clare, I'd better be going. Don't bother to mention I came."

"Well," the incorrigible Mrs. Brown said, "if it's Alison you're interested in, young fella, you'll have to look sharp! All the chaps are after her!"

"That isn't true, Mrs. Brown, and if you don't know where my sister can be found, will you excuse us? Do come into the house, Keith," she begged. "I'd like a word with you."

He followed her rather reluctantly.

"Oh, that awful woman!" Clare exploded, shutting the door. "She puts the wrong construction on everything."

"*Is* it the wrong construction?"

"Yes, Keith, it is," Clare said firmly. "It's Dr. Shaw, the man I work for. To be honest, I lost my temper this morning and our voices were raised, and his father came in and told us to shut up (we're all old friends—you probably know the Shaws know our cousin Susan awfully well!) and he said I was to go with his son on the rounds while he took surgery. I should have gone."

"Why didn't you, Clare?"

She hunched her shoulders. "It's a ghastly mess, to tell you the truth. I'm sort of engaged to the other man I work for— that Mrs. Brown mentioned him—it isn't official and I don't want him, but what's the use when you're silly over someone who just doesn't see you?"

"This Dr. Shaw who has taken Alison out this morning?" Keith suggested, trying to follow the story.

Clare nodded. "I don't want Alison to know. I don't know quite why. I did try to tell her, but the children messed it up by repeating something they'd heard me say to their mother, only they thought I was referring to Ewan Burnett, so Alison rather pushed me his way, thinking she was helping."

"Because she's getting interested in Shaw?" he suggested, painfully.

"No! No, she isn't—at least, I'm sure

she isn't! He likes her a lot, but he's just a family friend in her eyes, I'm sure. Oh, I'm telling this awfully badly. You see, *I* believe she's terribly unhappy because of this row with you, and she doesn't want my life to be messed up, so she's—"

"No, I won't buy that," he broke in, firmly.

"You're both so adamant, and I think you're both so wrong," Clare told him. "I believe you telephoned her one night while I was out. I found her crying. She wouldn't tell me why. The children said you'd been on the phone."

He turned away. "Yes, I know. I tried to explain to her what that girl meant to me but she wouldn't listen."

"The medical student? The one who was in the car with you?"

"Alison told you about that?" he cried.

"It's about all she told me, except that she was trying to accept that you'd go for an extremely pretty girl. Alison thinks she's plain, you see."

"I know, I *know!* I've had all this out with her but it's no use. All right, I was driving Zoë in my car. I have done before —I'm likely to again."

"Is that wise?"

"She's a friend. Her brother and I were at school together. Now he's in Africa and she doesn't know anyone else so she turns to me—naturally."

"Oh, one of those! It's no use, Keith. It isn't likely that any girl would accept that from her man."

"But it's true! I tried to explain to Alison. On the phone—in my letters. I wasn't hiding anything. Well, if she won't accept it, there it is. I'm not going to turn my back on Zoë just because Alison is being difficult. I love Alison as I always did, and Zoë is just the sister of my old friend."

"Then you'll wait for Alison?" Clare said quietly. "Don't look so outraged, Keith. If you want her to accept that you go out with Zoë in the car, why can't you accept that she's only accepting a lift from the doctor?"

"That's different, especially after all the things that Mrs. Brown said, and suggested."

"She's just a gossip. She always makes something out of everything," Clare urged.

He stood and thought, then shook his head. "No, it won't do, Clare. If Alison changes her mind, then the next move must come from her."

There was nothing Clare could do to dissuade him in this attitude, so she let him go.

As no one else seemed to know where Alison was, Clare left a note for her that she wouldn't be in for lunch. Raymond must have come here straight after she herself left the surgery. Probably to continue the argument they had been having. He couldn't have known Clare would go to the hairdresser's, but if he found Alison going out with the children it seemed the most natural thing in the world for him to offer Alison a lift.

She caught a bus to Monks Haybury, and found, in the newspaper offices, a very helpful old clerk who insisted on finding the story for her.

"As a matter of fact, I was looking at it myself, only the other day," he said. "I saw the chap, you see. He's a right one!"

"How do you mean?" Clare asked, keeping her eyes on the page. It was a bad photograph of Ewan, and it made him look quite different. Ruthless, hard, uncaring.

"Well, he's rolling in money, and no one's going to tell me strings weren't pulled. Of course it was his fault! I know someone who saw it happen, but there were other witnesses who said it wasn't his fault. And what did he get? His licence suspended. And now he's driving again. Saw the car myself—a real beauty. Wonder how long it'll stay like that?"

"He's a very careful driver, I believe," Clare ventured.

"Is he a friend of yours?"

"I work for him," she said briefly. "But I hadn't heard this story till today, in the hairdresser's. I couldn't believe it was true. What about the scandal over that girl?"

The clerk withdrew. "I didn't know you worked for him. It's all there—you read it, and make of it what you like. I've said too much already."

Having said that, he took himself off to get a cup of tea, but he had made his point. Try as she would, Clare couldn't convince herself that Ewan had come out well from that story in the newspaper, either.

She sighed, and went to get a snack lunch. She had to go to Wycherley Holt to work this afternoon as if nothing had happened.

Well, had anything happened? How did it affect her, she reasoned? She was standing in as Ewan's fiancée, as part of her job, and it would be broken off later. What did it matter, then, what had happened almost two years ago? And in any case, if Alison was going to stay here, and the doctor persuaded her to marry him, being paired with Ewan would have its face-saving qualities, Clare thought ruefully.

What, she asked herself, would Alison really do? Almost half of that month had gone by, and she had said nothing of her intentions at the end of that holiday. In Clare's heart had been cherished the hope that her sister would patch it up with Keith and go back, but now that didn't seem likely.

She telephoned Ewan at the bus station, to tell him she might be a little late, but he told her not to come in. "I've been trying to phone you at home, Clare, but no one seems to be in. Dear Mrs. Hewitt has threatened to descend on me this afternoon, so I'm going to be out. There's something I have to do in London, which is a good excuse."

He waited, obviously expecting her to ask him what it was, but now Clare was becoming really worried about Alison. Where could she have got to? She should have been back long ago with the children. Had something happened?

She said goodbye to the disappointed Ewan and hurried to catch her bus, but the phone call had delayed her and she just saw it moving off as she ran into the bus terminus. That meant half an hour to wait.

She employed the time telephoning to the doctor's house. If he weren't back either, it would mean that he had taken Alison and the children with him, she hoped. But Raymond Shaw was back.

"Alison? No, I don't know where she is, Clare. You seem to think I know all her movements! What is more to the point, where were you this morning? I went to your home but you weren't there!"

"Never mind me," she said impatiently.

"Alison ought to have been back long ago, but she isn't. She wasn't there when I returned this morning, and a neighbour said she went off with you in your car."

"I gave her a lift to the shops," he said coldly. "Mellie was rather cross—probably developing a cold. Don't worry, I'll look in on them tonight as usual. Now, about you, Clare—"

"I'm in Monks Haybury. I've just telephoned Ewan to say I'll be late and he said he doesn't want me this afternoon. The whole point is, he'd tried to telephone the house to tell someone, to stop me coming, and there was no one there, and there ought to have been! Where *is* Alison?"

"With the children somewhere, I imagine. Stop fussing, my dear. Alison is extremely capable with those children, and she'll know what to do with Mellie. Children are always tiresome when they've small ailments."

"I know Alison is wonderful with children," she said patiently. "And she wouldn't over-run their lunch—"

"Clare, she's probably taken them out to lunch. About you, Clare—have you left me, or were you just in a temper? If so, how long will it be before I can expect you at the surgery again?"

"Oh, you are exasperating! I rang you to help me. I've lost my bus so I shall be half an hour later getting home to find out for myself what has happened."

"I'll come and pick you up," he said at once.

"No, I don't want you to pick me up. I just want to know what's happened to Alison!"

"All right, I'll drive over to the house and see if she's there, but how will that help you?"

"I don't know," Clare said, and to her disgust she sounded near to tears.

He could hear that too, at the other end, and he didn't know what to do. She was so proud and independent. She'd only lose her temper again if he said anything and betrayed that he knew she was nearly crying. So he said instead, "What are you doing in Monks Haybury—or shouldn't I ask?"

"I went to check up on that rumour you were so pleased to relay to me about Ewan," she said, her anxiety making her sound angry.

"Oh. And what did you find?"

"I read the story for myself. Both stories, to be precise. So now I know all the facts."

"And—" He sounded so cool, amused almost, that she really did lose her temper. She longed to be there to hit out at him.

"And it doesn't matter a bit to me!" she flared and slammed down the receiver.

She put her hot forehead against the glass of the kiosk. What did she do a thing like that for, speaking to him like that? Why couldn't she be nice to him? She was, after all, asking him a favour.

But he managed to make her so nettled that she couldn't think straight these days when she was talking to him. She thought about it all the way back to the bus queue and all the way home, and as she neared Susan's house her anxious thoughts switched to Alison and the children. She found herself praying they would be there, and be all right.

Alison was going up the stairs when Clare opened the door. She looked white and strained.

"Alison! There you are! Where were

you? I've been so worried!" Clare exclaimed.

Alison put her finger to her lips and looked up the stairs. "Keep your voice down, Clare. It's Mellie."

"What's wrong now?"

Alison came back. "Her temperature's up again. She wasn't well, but we had to go out shopping. She was sick and I couldn't find a taxi."

"But Raymond was with you."

"No, this was some time after he dropped us at the shops. Anyway, he went on the rounds then. Mr. Kelly in the chemists said if I liked to wait there with her, he'd run us home at lunch-time, only she was sick, so his wife took us upstairs to her flat and Mellie went to sleep and we didn't disturb her. They haven't got any children and they dote on them."

"Yes, but that was lunch-time. Where have you been since then?"

"He couldn't get his car to start. Oh, time went on. I don't know. Finally he did bring us. Now I've got her in bed, and Raymond's coming back later."

"He's been?"

Alison nodded, as if it were the most

natural thing in the world that he should come over right away. Well, of course, it was, wasn't it, Clare reminded herself.

She flopped on to a chair. "Anything I can do?"

"No, not really. Everything under control."

Alison went on upstairs, her thoughts bound up with the children, Raymond. She hadn't asked Clare what she was doing at home or where she had been—but of course, if Raymond had already been here, he would have told her.

She went up to look at Mellie a little later. Alison kept her back from the cot, in case she disturbed her.

The child looked odd; her eyes were red and hot looking, and she looked hot, yet her little face was white. Her usual cheeky expression was no longer there. There was such a heavy look about those usually sparkling wide eyes that Clare felt a lump come into her throat.

She found Jayne in her room crying softly over the postcards that had come from Susan and Tony.

"Jayne! What is it, honey?" Clare said, picking her up and putting her on her lap.

Jayne didn't resist, but her little body was tensed against the comforting embrace Clare offered her. "What is it, sweetie? Tell Clare."

Jayne shook her head fiercely.

"Then if I call Alison, will you tell her?" Clare offered, anxiously. Jayne usually let her hug her when Alison was preoccupied with Mellie.

Jayne hesitated, then shook her head.

"Well, Raymond's coming again soon. Will you tell him?" Clare persevered.

Again Jayne shook her head.

She held the postcards up against her face, and then tried to stuff them down the neck of her jersey.

"What are you doing with those, you silly baby?" Clare laughed, and tried to take them away from her. "You'll scratch your neck with them, silly!"

Jayne screamed.

Alison came running in. "Oh, Clare, what *is* going on? Don't let her make a noise—come out and leave her, if you can't keep her quiet!"

She took Jayne off Clare's lap and carried her downstairs. "I'd better give you something to eat. You'd like some nice milk, wouldn't you? Don't worry about Mellie. I expect it's just a cold. You'll be the next, I expect. Let me feel your head."

Clare heard Alison's comforting small talk all the way down the stairs.

She went into her room and put on fresh make-up. When she went downstairs, Jayne was placidly eating her tea, alone, at the kitchen table. She stopped eating and looked guardedly at Clare, in the doorway. Clare turned away and the child began eating again.

Raymond came over after Jayne had been put to bed. Alison had had to send for him. Mellie's temperature was still rising. They were both worried about the child.

"What is wrong with her?" she asked them both, as they came down the stairs talking quietly.

"It's an infection," he said, very seriously. It was the same sort of thing he said to relatives of the patients, who didn't know anything about it and were vaguely comforted by his tones. It usually meant he hadn't been able to arrive at a diagnosis. Clare was surprised he should say that to her. She almost smiled at the incongruity of it, but he just hadn't noticed. He had turned back to Alison, and was giving her instructions.

The door-bell pealed suddenly. A tall figure loomed up outside, vaguely outlined behind the frosted glass panel. Mellie, hearing the noise, started to wail.

Clare opened the door. It was Keith Everton back again. She had forgotten all about him.

Looking past Clare, Keith stepped inside the hall, his face lighting up in spite of himself. "Alison—" he began.

Mellie's wails grew louder. Raymond turned to go up the stairs, Alison after him.

Then she must have realised who it was in the open doorway. "Not now, Keith!" Alison said distractedly. "Go away! I told you—" and without realising what she had done, she looked up into Raymond's face and followed him upstairs.

Keith hesitated. He averted his stricken face from Clare's gaze. "The children—" she began, in explanation, but he didn't wait to hear. He turned and walked out.

13

MELLIE didn't get any better. Clare got extended time off from Wycherley Holt, but Alison insisted that she should help at the surgery, where the situation had changed. Old Dr. Shaw himself wasn't so well, so the whole of the work fell on to Raymond's shoulders, and he now really needed Clare.

Around the third day of Mellie's illness, she complained of ear-ache. Raymond joyfully leapt on it, and examining her thoroughly, announced that it was her old middle-ear trouble.

"That's as badly inflamed a drum as I've seen for a long time!" he announced.

Alison nodded, a trace of relief in her face. She knew only too well from her work in a children's hospital, how happy the doctor was when he could at last see what was wrong, but to Clare, waiting near the door in case they needed something brought from the bathroom or kitchen, it seemed rather heartless. She only saw the surgery visits, not half way through the illness.

"You don't have to look so pleased about it, do you?" she murmured, in an outraged voice.

"Don't I!" he retorted. "Now we can pump some antibiotics into her, and this little scrap should be on her feet in no time —or almost no time."

Clare took the prescription to the chemist and waited while it was made up.

Sitting in the chemist's shop watching people coming and going, weighing babies on the wicker basket of the big scale, buying tins of baby foods and cosmetics, people without a care in the world, she wondered what she ought to do. There was Alison, and Keith: not a word had passed Alison's lips about his visit, these last few days. Had she really been so obsessed with Mellie's illness, or didn't she really care about him any more? Yet she had been crying last night, from her bed in Susan's room where she had taken herself since the child's illness began.

Then there was Susan: Clare was all for sending for her. They had now had more than half their holiday and might reasonably feel they ought to have been brought back, now something had gone really wrong. But Raymond said no, and so did Alison. Clare was over-ruled.

There was Ewan, too. He was being very good about giving her leave this time. No demurring whatever. But she ought to see him, she felt, and tell him how Mrs. Hewitt was talking so carelessly in the hairdresser's. Clare had heard whispers about it in other shops since then, and people looked speculatively at Clare herself.

She wondered what she would do about her visit to Monks Haybury, too. Should she tell Ewan she had looked up the old newspaper accounts? Or should she let things ride, and hope that the whole business of this phoney engagement would fizzle out, leaving her just his secretary? In that case, it really didn't matter very much either way.

She hurried back home with the medicine. Raymond had left a very small quantity he had brought with him for Alison to be getting on with, but she would need the rest of it soon.

Alison met her at the door. "Just getting a breath of fresh air," she said. "I gave Mellie her dose and she's asleep. First good sleep she's had for three days."

"Where's Jayne?"

"Resting, too. She seems very quiet. I hope she isn't going to sicken for something, but she hasn't a temperature, so I suppose I mustn't start looking for trouble."

"That doesn't sound like you, Alison!" Clare said sharply. "You didn't sleep well, did you?"

"What's that, to a nurse?" Alison retorted. "If I can't stand one or two interruptions in my night's sleep, how can I hope to go back to nursing again?"

It seemed a good enough opportunity to discuss that subject, so Clare made some tea, and when they were settled in armchairs with the door left open in case Mellie should wake, Clare said, tentatively, "Have you thought about going back to your old hospital, then?"

Alison closed her eyes, her face washed of all expression. "No. I haven't given the future a single thought, and I don't intend to until the day Sue and Tony come back, so don't raise the point again, there's a dear."

That seemed so definite that Clare was really worried. She knew better than to actually mention Keith's name. Alison in this weepy worried state would promptly fly off the handle and probably never go back to Keith. As it was, Clare thought there might be just a chance to bring them together again. In her heart she felt that whatever Raymond's feelings were, he wasn't right for Alison. Alison was, she believed, still in love with Keith, and he certainly was in love with her.

Whether he had been influenced too far, by Mrs. Brown's innuendo about the doctor, when he saw him there with Alison and she had so abruptly dismissed Keith, Clare had no idea. She could only try.

Raymond was taking evening surgery, and had asked Clare if she minded coming just for that evening. Alison said at once, "You go, Clare, of course. I'll manage all right. Jayne will be in bed by then."

On the way to the surgery, Clare made up her mind to telephone Keith at his hospital.

As it happened, they caught him just as

he was going off duty. He came unwillingly. She could hear the reluctance in his voice, once he knew who was calling him.

"Keith, it's Clare here," she said, without preamble. "I'm on my way to the surgery, where I work, but I had to try and speak to you. Alison has no idea I'm doing this."

"I don't understand," he said, and he didn't sound as if he were particularly interested.

"Keith, that day you came and Alison wasn't there, I wasn't expecting you back again, and Alison certainly wasn't—she didn't even know you'd called earlier. You took us all by surprise."

He didn't answer that, so she ploughed on with determination. "Keith, if only you could have let me know you were coming back! We were in the most awful state— Alison had been out alone with the children (the doctor *had* only given her a lift to the shops) and Mellie had been taken ill and she hadn't been able to get a cab. She was worried sick, and we didn't know what was wrong with Mellie."

"Never mind, Clare. Alison has her new doctor friend to help her. You don't have

268

to keep me briefed about her life to date. I'm not in it. You must have seen that for yourself," Keith said coldly.

"Keith, I could shake you! She was off her head with worry—she didn't know what she was saying."

"She's a children's nurse. She doesn't get shaken out of her stride easily. Besides, her manners are above average, so if Alison says she doesn't want to be bothered with someone's tiresome presence, you may take it that she does know what she's saying and that she really means it, in exactly the way she says it."

"But Keith—"

"Clare, my dear, I like you very much. You'd have made a corking good sister-in-law. But you have one failing. You will meddle, and other people's love affairs are not for you to fix. Now listen to me. I'm not a bad loser, I hope, and I know I've had my chips. For some reason Alison likes this other chap better than she likes me. Okay, good luck to him! But you let it rest there, Clare. Don't try to change things."

"Oh! You make me sick, Keith Everton! You're all wrong! You *are* a bad loser, and you've too much stiff-necked pride. If you want a thing (or a person) badly enough, you've got to keep on trying, not just retire gracefully at the first set-back. Besides, you and Alison have both got beastly bad tempers. I haven't patience with either of you. She wants you as badly as she wants anyone, but she won't admit it. But this I am sure of—she isn't in love with Raymond Shaw. I told you so, and everything she says and does points to that. But you won't take any notice of anything I say—I can see that! You want to go your own sweet way, having all your own way, and ruining two lives! Oh, I wish I hadn't bothered with you. Good-*bye*."

She slammed down the receiver, aware that her eyes were too misty for her to see herself in the little mirror above the telephone. Also aware that she was shaking all over and there was a hard lump in her throat that she couldn't swallow. She had made things worse than they were, and there was nothing left that she could do.

They had a rather full surgery that night, of really sick people. If they had to be run off their feet, Clare preferred this to the long stream of people who just wanted another bottle. She was hardly aware of the way the time flew, until the last patient came in and went, and surgery closed.

Then he stood up and stretched, smiling ruefully at her. "What a life!" he grinned; then he turned her round to the light and looked hard at her. "You're not sickening for something, are you, Clare? Stick your tongue out and let's have a look!"

"I will not!" she said indignantly. "There's nothing wrong with me that a good night's sleep won't cure. Perhaps we'll all get one now—young Mellie's sleeping her head off since you came today."

"Good! Are you working in the afternoons?" he asked delicately, managing not to have to mention Ewan's detested name, but not managing to disguise how distasteful the mere thought of the man was to him.

"I've got extended leave in the afternoons."

"I'm glad, Clare. I really am. I can't help feeling you were trying to do too much." He smoothed back his hair irritably. "All right, don't look at me like that. I know I manage to sound like your uncle, but there it is. I'll run you home in the car."

"I thought you weren't going to see Mellie tonight? You've got the Farrans to see, and they're in the other direction," she objected.

"I'll look in on Mellie, just the same," he said firmly.

In the car, she was strongly tempted to ask him what he thought about Alison, but if he were keen on Alison (as Clare believed him to be) then it would hardly be tactful to talk to him about Keith Everton. So she said nothing.

"How is Jayne behaving?" the doctor asked her. "Is she leading Alison a devil of a dance?"

"No, she isn't too bad . . . with Alison. It's me she leads a dance," she said, thinking of the episode of the postcards. But she didn't think it worth repeating to Raymond, and she was sorry for it later.

When they arrived at the house, he was glad he had decided to drop in on Mellie after all. The child's temperature was still soaring.

"Do you know where Susan is now?" he asked Alison. She shook her head.

"No, she said she'd let us know the new address but she hasn't yet." She thought a moment and then called softly to Clare. "Was that the name of the village or the house, that Susan was supposed to go to?" she asked her.

"La Fidelle des Roses? I've no idea," Clare said, frowning. "Why?"

Alison shook her head. "Raymond is asking."

"Is Mellie worse then?"

"She's no better," Alison said, after the slightest hesitation.

Raymond looked at their distressed faces. "Look, we'll give it another twenty-four hours, to give the antibiotics a chance, but then if she's no better, I think we shall have to try sending a cable to this place. But of course you might hear from Susan with her new address tomorrow morning. And don't come in to morning surgery, Clare—stay with your sister for a few days. Don't worry, either of you. If it comes to the worst, there's a chap I know —he's a London man and very good. I'll take the responsibility of calling him in, just for his advice. Remember that, both of you."

It was at Clare that he looked as he said it, but she was watching her sister's face, and wishing she had managed to get Keith to come and try to make it up with Alison. She was sure that Alison's strength would be fortified by the thought of Keith in her life again.

The next few days were to live in Clare's memory. Mellie's temperature fell a little, but she was still very ill. They did hear from Susan, but it was to say that they had moved on from that place. Lightheartedly Susan said they had no idea themselves where they would finish up, but not to worry—they had not much more than a week before they had to start thinking about the journey home, and she sent their love to the girls.

Raymond still came in twice a day, although he had the full weight of the practice on his shoulders. His father's gout added itself to his miseries, and the older man was furious to think he was penned to his room, unable to help.

Ewan telephoned one afternoon. Clare left the nursing to her sister, and ran the house. It was the thing she did best, and as Jayne had contracted a sniffly cold and was kept to her room, Alison managed very well, teetering between the two children. It was only Alison they wanted, and no matter how ill Mellie seemed to be, she managed to croak, "Want Ally—Ally not leave Mellie."

Ewan said, without preamble, "Clare, are you alone? Able to talk private and personal?"

"Yes, Ewan," she said, wondering what on earth he had to say.

"Remember I went to London that day to avoid our friend?"

"Yes. Did you?"

"That day, yes, but she came unannounced the day afterwards. Clare, I don't know how to say this, but she's been telling me the oddest story about you! I was furious with her, of course, but she assured me that she was only repeating what she had heard, and that as we seemed to be very friendly, you and I, she thought I ought to know."

Clare was flabbergasted. "She did *what?* What did she say about me?"

"Clare, you did tell me that there was

no one else in your life, or I wouldn't have entertained this idea from the first."

"What did she *say*, Ewan?"

"Well, it wasn't what she said, so much as what she was trying not to tell me other people had said. It seems that people are saying that you had a gentleman friend, a doctor, with you in your home the other day."

"Gentleman friend!" she said in disgust. "Really Ewan—you know Dr. Shaw, and you know why he haunts our house— young Mellie is terribly ill. A doctor doesn't visit the house twice a day for fun! Tell your friend Mrs. Hewitt so!"

"Clare, I didn't mean Shaw. Of course I know Shaw and why he is visiting. This was another doctor, from London."

"Doctor from London?" Clare repeated, uncomprehending. Then she realised who he must mean! "Good gracious—that was my sister Alison's fiancé! How did Mrs. Hewitt know he was a doctor? He isn't qualified yet, but that's by the way."

"Mrs. Hewitt didn't know. She heard that you were both very intense about something, and embarrassed when a neighbour came along and spoke."

"Mrs. Hewitt must be employing a detective to watch every move I make, if she has found out that much!" Clare said angrily.

"Really, Clare, that is most uncalled for! Of course Mrs. Hewitt isn't employing a detective. She wouldn't sink so low."

"Oh, what are we going on like this for? Ewan, dear Ewan, I didn't really mean that! Of course I know she wouldn't. I was just frustrated and flummoxed wondering how on earth she could have found out so much. I didn't expect Keith to come—it was unexpected. He couldn't wait, so I tried to tell him how unhappy my sister was about him—of course we looked intense. It was terribly important and a painful subject we were discussing. Of course we might have looked embarrassed by that neighbour appearing—she's a very inquisitive person and a mischief maker. In three short minutes she'd said enough, or suggested enough, to undo all I'd been doing, and to give him the impression my sister didn't want him any more! He took himself off, and I could candidly have hit her. Now are you satisfied?"

"I don't know, Clare. Mrs. Hewitt was

distressed about it. She was very convincing, too!"

"Ewan, you believe her and not me!" Clare said, scandalised, and then she saw, to her horror, that Alison was standing in the doorway, listening to all that.

It put her mind off what she had intended to tell Ewan about what she had heard Mrs. Hewitt say in the hairdresser's. All she could think of at that moment was that Alison was hearing for the first time that Keith had visited the house, Clare had tried to persuade him to come back to her, an inquisitive neighbour had interrupted and presumably heard it all or most of it, and that Clare herself was recounting it to Ewan.

"I can't stop now, Ewan," she said, hardly noticing what he was saying to her. "I'll call you back. We have illness in the house, remember?" In that moment she didn't care how brusque she was with him. It wasn't the important thing. The really important thing was to catch Alison and straighten this whole matter up before it got out of hand.

Alison had turned and was going upstairs again.

"Alison! Let me explain," Clare begged. "I wanted to tell you, but there hasn't been the right time to get you quietly and when I did try to tell you, you shut your eyes and said you didn't want to talk about him."

Alison paused on the stairs and looked frostily down at her sister. "I didn't think you were like that, Clare—I thought you were kind and could be trusted. I didn't think you'd talk to everyone else about something that was my affair, and mine only."

Clare was stricken silent. Not only by Alison's choice of words, but that new hostility in her sister's eyes.

14

HOW had Mrs. Lattimore Hewitt discovered about it in the first place, Clare asked herself, as she finished her house-cleaning, and put on some lunch for Alison and herself?

Someone appeared at the window, gently tapping at the glass. It was Mrs. Brown again, holding up an empty coffee tin.

"Oh, *no!*" Clare murmured, and went to the door.

"I'll just pop in to see how the children are, dear," Mrs. Brown said, thrusting forward, "and then I'll borrow a bit of coffee, if you don't mind, just to save me from going to the shops."

Clare stood her ground. Mrs. Brown pulled up in surprise. "Aren't you going to ask me in, Clare? Don't mind me—I've seen people in their housework overall before now, dear!"

"I can't ask you in, Mrs. Brown," Clare said levelly, "and I can't lend you any coffee. But I would like to ask you if you saw an elderly woman, a very smartly dressed woman, enquiring for me. Did you speak to her? Her name is Mrs. Lattimore Hewitt."

"Well, of course I didn't! Anyone would think I spent my time watching who came to your door! What a thing to suggest!" Mrs. Brown blustered, and decided to leave without waiting to borrow the coffee. But from her expression Clare was sure it was Mrs. Brown who had talked to Ewan's friend.

"If you must talk to strangers about me, be sure you get your facts right!" Clare said angrily to Mrs. Brown's back view. "You don't know what harm you might do!"

"I shall tell your cousin, when she comes home, that you are rude and ill-mannered and—I shall tell her all about your goings-on, miss!" Mrs. Brown said, raising her voice angrily, as she slammed the gate to.

Alison came to the head of the stairs and looked down. "Who was that at the door, Clare?"

"It was only Mrs. Brown, came to

borrow coffee, but she went without it. I don't think she'll come to borrow anything else," Clare said.

Alison nodded and went back to Mellie's cot. The child was whimpering again, and very restless.

"What could be the matter with her?" Clare asked herself, and thought of the childish ailments she had seen the start of, in the surgery. But most of Raymond's little patients had measles and other childish complaints. There was, of course, mastoid, but Mellie had stopped putting her hand to her ear. Raymond said the condition was clearing up quickly, but Mellie herself wasn't responding to the drugs.

The telephone rang and Clare answered it with a sigh. It was going to be one of those days.

It was Dr. Shaw's father. "Is that you, Clare, m'dear?" he said, straight away. "I'm in a devil of a pickle. Gout's got me penned to my armchair. I can just about reach the telephone, but that's the lot, and I've just had a call that something ought to be done about, but I can't find my son. Do you know where he is?"

"No, I don't. I don't know his movements now I don't go to the surgery, you know. I suppose you can't ask Mrs. Rigg to go and look at the card index, or the appointments pad?"

"Mrs. Rigg's out, dash it! And it wouldn't be any good anyway, my girl. Since you've been away, the card index has gone to pot! As for the appointments pad, my son jots down things on bits of paper and loses 'em. Clare, I didn't mean it when I said we could do without you. We can't. I said it to jerk some sense into the heads of both of you."

"Sense, Dr. Shaw? I don't understand."

"Never mind, never mind. This is too urgent. Dash, what shall I do now? I hoped that Raymond might have said where he was going, when he looked in to see the children. Oh, well, I'll just have to keep phoning round, I suppose."

"What is it? Is there anything *I* can do?"

"I don't know, Clare. I'm a bit in the dark. The call came from the farm— Foxgate. We get a good many false alarms from there, and we get emergencies that shouldn't have happened. But this was a child's voice. Couldn't make head or tail of what was being said, though."

"How would you like me to pop up there, Dr. Shaw? I know Raymond was very anxious about that old boiler. Funny it wasn't the farmer or his wife, though."

"You! How would you go—the bus doesn't go near there!"

"The old bike—no, I know! I'll call Willy Tunks and see if he's going that way. He'll give me a lift."

"I'm much obliged to you, Clare. Ring me back and let's know what's happening, will you? And if nothing's really wrong, just tell 'em—well, you know what to tell them."

He hung up and Clare went to tell Alison what she was going to do. Alison was still rather frosty, but agreed that something ought to be done. "He must have closed surgery on the dot this morning, to be out on his rounds already," she murmured, half to herself. "Wonder why he didn't tell his father where he could be found?"

"I'll ring Willy Tunks," Clare said, refraining from passing on to Alison the news that there was now no efficiency or order at the doctors' now she herself wasn't there. That sort of communication would be no help at all, at the time, though not long ago Alison would have appreciated the joke.

Willy Tunks was delivering beyond the farm and said he'd call at once for Clare.

"Miss your cousin and her car, don't you, Miss Drury?" Willy asked, when he arrived and cleared a place for her beside the driver's seat. "You ought to learn to drive yourself, though I suppose you will when you and that Mr. Burnett—" and he paused delicately. His face was friendly, yet avid for news. "Everyone's talking about it."

"Never mind that, Willy," she said quickly. "The thing is, I called you in to help because this is an emergency for old Dr. Shaw," and she told him briefly about the phone call and the child's voice. "We couldn't waste time trying to contact Dr. Raymond Shaw so—"

"He couldn't have come, anyway," Willy said. "Just seen him myself, caught up with an accident on the bypass. Busy as anything, he was, cleaning up the injured and answering police questions.

285

Wouldn't have done to mention Foxgate to him, not at that moment, seeing as how he do go on rare about the folk up at the farm."

Clare suppressed a smile. Willy knew everyone and everything that was going on in Rexmundham and felt a family interest in them all. His views on the people at Foxgate were stronger, if anything, than those of Raymond Shaw.

The farm was quiet when they arrived. Ominously quiet. "Where *are* they all, then?" Willy said blankly.

"Come on, we must hurry!" Clare said, getting out, Willy at her heels.

One of the boys came running up. Dirty, his shirt torn, his voice high with anxiety. His arms and legs were blood-stained. He was twelve, thin, under-sized, with the small eyes of his father, and the pasty skin of his mother. He looked at Clare, and at Willy Tunks, wildly, unbelieving. "Where's the doctor, then? I did phone him—it's me Dad. Why don't he come, then—it'll be too late. Me Dad's down the old well!"

So that was it. Clare cast a despairing look at Willy Tunks, who promptly ran after the boy, up the field to where the well—now only a half dried up shaft—had lasted too long with nothing but a rotten cover over the low surrounding wall. Half the district had been on to the farmer to do something about it for years, because of the danger to hikers who used the old footpath across his land.

Clare didn't wait. She ran into the house and telephoned old Dr. Shaw to tell him what had happened, and to let him know where Raymond had been when Willy saw him.

"Tell them not to try to get him up—I'll lay on an ambulance, Clare. Round up his wife and the others to stand by."

The woman was up at the well with the rest of the hands, who were ineffectually trying to get ropes down. She relayed her message. The farmer was injured. He lay there swearing up at them, cursing his leg, his back, his head, and shouting at them to leave him there to die.

"Come back to the farm," Clare urged his wife, "I want to get your boy cleaned up. How did he get like that?"

"Helping his dad—or trying to. I don't know what'll become of us. All very fine the doctor saying we ought to get all this put right, but the farm don't pay as it is. Repairs cost money."

"But you've more sons—grown-up ones —why don't they all help? Even home repairs are better than letting things get dangerous," Clare said vigorously as she led the woman back and prised the boy away from the group. "Now you let me clean up those places on your arms and legs," Clare told him. "There's an ambulance coming for your father, and the emergency services. They'll soon have him out."

The woman kept on grumbling in her despairing monotone. "No hot water this morning. The boiler's playing up. And I can't get the range to steam up enough for even a kettle. Nothing's right, and Denks is in that bad a mood, I daren't ask him to do it."

Clare had washed the boy's wounds in cold water and the last drop of disinfectant the farm boasted in its very inadequate first aid box when the ambulance arrived. She had managed to coax the farmer's wife to stoke the boiler having admitted she knew how to do it but didn't dare touch it. It was growling and glowing when Clare looked into the boiler-house.

"It shouldn't be making that noise!" the woman said, fearfully.

"Who can we ask to help us with it? Where are all the others?" Clare asked. "Go and fetch them—they'll be in the way at the well!"

It then transpired that two of the older sons had quarrelled with their father that morning, and taken themselves up to the Black Spinney to mend a fence. The confusion was mounting with the arrival of the men with the tackle. Clare called Willy Tunks.

"Do *you* know anything about boilers like this one, Willy?"

He shook his head. "And I wouldn't go near it. I don't like the look of it. Tell you what, I'll go and pull out one of them gawping chaps as ought to be in the milking shed by rights. Back in a jiff— and keep her out of the boiler-house," he said, jerking a thumb at the ineffectual Mrs. Denks.

Clare had never seen a farmer's wife who looked so lost and bewildered. "You'd better come in the kitchen while I make you a cup of tea," she said. It occurred to her that the woman might be ill, and not just suffering from the shock of seeing her husband in such a predicament.

They had just left the boiler-house when there was a sudden roar and a crash, and hot water hissed and spurted everywhere.

"Oh, my lor, that's the boiler burst!" Mrs. Denks shouted. Then she screamed, "Where's Dick? Little Dick—he went back after the cat! I saw him!"

Willy Tunks came back. "Are you all all right? That was a nasty turn—I thought you were still in there. Here, get as far away as you can—that's going to burn! There she goes!"

Others were running back from the well. They streamed over the grass and down the hill. The ambulance began to pick its way down the rutted place that served as a private drive to the farm and made Raymond Shaw so angry. The men with the tackle came and Clare told one of them what had happened.

Willy held on to her. "You're not going back in there! That kid wouldn't be daft enough to stay in with the boiler making a row like that! He's away into the house by now."

"Please look, Willy, while I call for the fire brigade," Clare gasped.

Smoke was everywhere, and more shouting and confusion. When she reached the telephone, she found the line was dead. There was nothing for it but to organise a human chain of buckets, if they wanted to save the farm.

Willy Tunks had found the boy, and someone else was holding on to Mrs. Denks. Clare gave directions, and the men did as she asked them. Just over the hill was Haggett Lodge, another farm, an efficient one. Clare sent someone over to find fire extinguishers. Someone else was set to removing the farmers' papers from the room they called the study. Nothing was in order in there, but at least they wouldn't lose their insurance papers and other valuables.

Ben, one of the older sons, said worriedly, "It's going to spread to the main house, sure as eggs is eggs. If only that old barn weren't there."

"It looks rickety enough to fall down," Clare said crisply. "If I were a man, I'd drive something heavy against it and knock it down. At least it would stop the fire spreading."

Denks' family weren't used to having clear orders rapped out at them. They only knew their father's grumbling and swearing. Clare hadn't meant to give an order—she didn't know much about such things, but it seemed logical, and she was tired of all these grown people standing helplessly around until someone told them what to do. To her surprise, Joe Denks raced over to the next barn for the tractor, his other brother with him. The rickety connecting building caved in with a roar and a cloud of smoke.

Out of the nightmare, someone said, "Young Dr. Shaw's coming up the drive now." Clare heard them, and then someone else said, "It's that cat again—up there at the window. The kid's gone up after it."

Clare had been haunted by that boy and his thin face and anxious little eyes. A child brought up without love. It was natural that he should pin his affection to an animal. As she heard it said, she saw a hand come to the window and try to pluck

292

the frightened animal down from where it crouched on the edge of the frame. A child's thin hand.

"It is—it's the boy! Go in and get him!" Clare said to big Joe.

"Where, miss? I don't see nothing at the window, only smoke!" he protested. "Now look, miss, no use looking at me like that! There's nothing there! You've chased us all around and got things in order and that's fine by me, but you're not getting me into that place on a wild goose chase! Why, the whole shindy'll fall down any minute—me father's let it go to such rack and ruin."

"Then I'll go myself," Clare muttered.

Someone tried to stop her, but there was such a noise everywhere. Inside the house it was dark and smoke-filled. In spite of knocking down the intersecting building, the house had caught, at the back where the cat was. She stumbled up the rickety staircases, silently cursing Farmer Denks and his cheese-paring and muddled ways.

The boy had got the cat by now, and had hidden its face under his coat.

Clare tore off her jacket and put it over

his head. "Hold it over your face, and run!" she said.

He took the hint and went helter-skelter down the stairs. She followed closely, but on the way a door burst open and a cloud of smoke came out. It blocked her sight and she slipped, and her foot went through the rotten wood stair. She felt herself falling, and her head struck something . . .

Clare was in hospital for three weeks. During that time, many things happened, among them the return of Susan and Tony. But Raymond Shaw never seemed to bother even to ask how she was.

Susan was like a whirlwind in her visiting times—full of her holiday, and apparently unaware of their acute anxiety over Mellie.

"I knew it would happen, Clare," Susan said, quite calmly. "That's why I only left her because it was Alison taking over—I knew Mellie would fret herself sick with anyone else. But I suppose having two duckings in the water, and ear trouble as well was a bit much for the poor mite. Anyway, she's all right now."

"All right" meant that Mellie was sitting

up in bed taking a little food, but before Clare was out of hospital Mellie was up and about and had had other but less disastrous adventures.

"You've been concussed—we're not to worry you with excitements," Susan usually said on her visits, and then promptly spilled more news, the best being Alison's return to Keith Everton.

"Apparently you ticked him off on the telephone the day before your fun at the farm, Clare, so he was full of remorse and came straight down to Rexmundham, and he's been at Alison's side ever since. I don't know what she would have done without him, old Dr. Shaw being laid up like that."

"You're forgetting—she had Raymond," Clare objected, but Susan looked bothered, and rushed on to some other news.

Clare noticed on many occasions that any mention of Raymond Shaw was brushed aside quickly. One day she tackled Susan about it.

"He might have at least looked in to see how I was," she said, in a hurt voice. "He has to look in on his other patients."

"Oh, help, I promised him I wouldn't tell you but I can't have you thinking such things about him. Anyway, he should be well enough to come over and see you for himself soon, so here goes. Yes, well enough! The poor darling saw you go into the farmhouse, and went mad! He just ran in after you. If it hadn't been for him, when you got stuck in that staircase—" and she trailed off miserably.

Clare was struggling up in bed. It didn't matter that Ewan had sent no flowers or even messages—that was understandable, since the nurses had been talking about Mr. Burnett going on a sudden visit abroad for his work. Clare had expected something of the sort, after that frigid telephone conversation with him that day. But it mattered very much about Raymond.

"What happened to him?" she choked.

"Well, part of the building fell on him, but don't worry—he was lucky! He hurt both his legs, but he'll be *all right*."

Clare wouldn't give anyone any peace, then, until she was allowed to see him. As his legs were still elevated, and unable to move, she had to be wheeled over to him in a chair. Two lift rides and across the connecting bridge between the male and female wings of the hospital made her feel decidedly queazy by the time she reached his bedside, and she knew by the way he looked critically at her that he was well aware she wasn't really fit for this effort, but that didn't matter.

"I had to see you, Raymond!" she gasped.

"Oh, damn, damn, damn," he said softly. "I was praying they'd stall you off asking, until I was ready to be let down off my pulleys to come and see *you!*" he said, but he reached forward and grabbed her hand and held on to it so tightly that she winced. "My dear girl, how *are* you?"

"I'm . . . not too bad!" she said, and to her dying shame, she couldn't speak any more, and put the other hand up to her face.

"Push her closer, nurse," he said savagely, "and then clear out of my room so we can talk!"

The nurse smiled understandingly and left them. Raymond could just about manage to put one arm round Clare, and they clung together.

When she could speak, she said, "Why did you do it? Why? I was managing and there were loads more people who could have come and helped me, who could have been *spared*. But you—a doctor—people *need* you—"

His face was a study. "Do you think I'd trust rescuing you, to anyone else?" he said thickly, and pulled her to him again.

A little later on, when they were both under control, he said, "Oh, Clare, what am I going to do about you?"

"What do you mean?"

"You're such an independent soul, but you need me, you know you do. Why don't you give in? What are you holding out for? Burnett's no good to you—he's gone abroad. Did you know that?"

She nodded. "But I thought you were keen on my sister; well, you can't blame me. You were always going to the house to see her—"

"To keep an eye on the children. It was a responsibility, with your cousin away, and I didn't want you worried more than need be. But then you started going out with Burnett. Clare, did you really care for him?"

She shook her head. "There's never been anyone else but you, Raymond, but you never seemed to need me. I wasn't any good with the children, and I know you thought a lot of Alison because of her gift of coping with them."

"My dear, good girl, if you'd been a perfect goose at everything, it wouldn't have mattered. It was you, all the way along the line. But it so happens you're the most efficient person I know, and what more could a doctor ask in a wife. You *will* marry me, I suppose?" he asked comically. "Of course, we can't approach the altar while I'm like this, and you don't look too glamorous yourself, my sweet, but as soon as we're okay, will you?"

She couldn't speak, but she nodded, vigorously, and he kissed her again.

Then the nurse came back. "I must take her away, Dr. Shaw, or Sister will give me a rocket," she said.

"You can take her for now, but I shall want to see her again, soon, so I know she's not running out on me," he said, with pretended ferocity and a rather shaky voice.

"I shan't," Clare promised, as she was wheeled away. "You need a secretary as well, so either way, you're stuck with me for life!"

THE END

GUIDE
TO THE COLOUR CODING
OF
ULVERSCROFT BOOKS

Many of our readers have written to us expressing their appreciation for the way in which our colour coding has assisted them in selecting the Ulverscroft books of their choice.

To remind everyone of our colour coding—this is as follows:

BLACK COVERS
Mysteries

*

BLUE COVERS
Romances

*

RED COVERS
Adventure Suspense and General Fiction

*

ORANGE COVERS
Westerns

*

GREEN COVERS
Non-Fiction

ROMANCE TITLES
in the
Ulverscroft Large Print Series

THE SHADOWS
OF THE CROWN TITLES
in the
Ulverscroft Large Print Series

FICTION TITLES
in the
Ulverscroft Large Print Series

The Onedin Line: The High Seas
Cyril Abraham

The Onedin Line: The Iron Ships
Cyril Abraham

The Onedin Line: The Shipmaster
Cyril Abraham

The Onedin Line: The Trade Winds
Cyril Abraham

The Enemy	*Desmond Bagley*
Flyaway	*Desmond Bagley*
The Master Idol	*Anthony Burton*
The Navigators	*Anthony Burton*
A Place to Stand	*Anthony Burton*
The Doomsday Carrier	*Victor Canning*
The Cinder Path	*Catherine Cookson*
The Girl	*Catherine Cookson*
The Invisible Cord	*Catherine Cookson*
Life and Mary Ann	*Catherine Cookson*
Maggie Rowan	*Catherine Cookson*
Marriage and Mary Ann	*Catherine Cookson*
Mary Ann's Angels	*Catherine Cookson*
All Over the Town	*R. F. Delderfield*
Jamaica Inn	*Daphne du Maurier*
My Cousin Rachel	*Daphne du Maurier*

MYSTERY TITLES
in the
Ulverscroft Large Print Series

Henrietta Who?	*Catherine Aird*
Slight Mourning	*Catherine Aird*
The China Governess	*Margery Allingham*
Coroner's Pidgin	*Margery Allingham*
Crime at Black Dudley	*Margery Allingham*
Look to the Lady	*Margery Allingham*
More Work for the Undertaker	
	Margery Allingham
Death in the Channel	*J. R. L. Anderson*
Death in the City	*J. R. L. Anderson*
Death on the Rocks	*J. R. L. Anderson*
A Sprig of Sea Lavender	*J. R. L. Anderson*
Death of a Poison-Tongue	*Josephine Bell*
Murder Adrift	*George Bellairs*
Strangers Among the Dead	*George Bellairs*
The Case of the Abominable Snowman	
	Nicholas Blake
The Widow's Cruise	*Nicholas Blake*
The Brides of Friedberg	*Gwendoline Butler*
Murder By Proxy	*Harry Carmichael*
Post Mortem	*Harry Carmichael*
Suicide Clause	*Harry Carmichael*
After the Funeral	*Agatha Christie*
The Body in the Library	*Agatha Christie*

NON-FICTION TITLES
in the
Ulverscroft Large Print Series